Lucky for Good

Also by Susan Patron

The Higher Power of Lucky
Lucky Breaks
Maybe Yes, Maybe No, Maybe Maybe

Lucky for Good

The final story in Lucky's Hard Pan Trilogy

by **susan patron**

with illustrations by **erin mcguire**

Atheneum Books for Young Readers
New York   London   Toronto
Sydney   New Delhi

ATHENEUM BOOKS FOR YOUNG READERS
An imprint of Simon & Schuster Children's Publishing Division
1230 Avenue of the Americas, New York, New York 10020
This book is a work of fiction. Any references to historical events, real people, or real locales are used fictitiously. Other names, characters, places, and incidents are products of the author's imagination, and any resemblance to actual events or locales or persons, living or dead, is entirely coincidental.
Text copyright © 2011 by Susan Patron
Illustrations copyright © 2011 by Erin McGuire
All rights reserved, including the right of reproduction in whole or in part in any form.
ATHENEUM BOOKS FOR YOUNG READERS is a registered trademark of Simon & Schuster, Inc.
For information about special discounts for bulk purchases, please contact Simon & Schuster Special Sales at 1-866-506-1949 or business@simonandschuster.com.
The Simon & Schuster Speakers Bureau can bring authors to your live event. For more information or to book an event, contact the Simon & Schuster Speakers Bureau at 1-866-248-3049 or visit our website at www.simonspeakers.com.
Also available in an Atheneum Books for Young Readers hardcover edition
Book design by Sonia Chaghatzbanian
The text for this book is set in Berkeley.
The illustrations for this book are rendered in pencil.
Manufactured in the United States of America
0712 OFF
First Atheneum Books for Young Readers paperback edition August 2012
10 9 8 7 6 5 4 3 2 1
The Library of Congress has cataloged the hardcover edition as follows:
Patron, Susan, 1948–
Lucky for good / Susan Patron; illustrated by Erin McGuire.—1st ed.
p. cm.
Summary: The residents of Hard Pan, California, come together to help Brigitte and Lucky when the County Health Department threatens to close down the Café, and in the meantime Miles's life is complicated by his mother's return.
ISBN 978-1-4169-9058-1 (hc)
[1. Restaurants—Fiction. 2. Interpersonal relations—Fiction. 3. Community life—California—Fiction. 4. Mothers and sons—Fiction. 5. Christian life—Fiction. 6. California—Fiction.] I. McGuire, Erin, ill. II. Title.
PZ7.P2765Lvf 2011
[Fic]—dc22   2010022040
ISBN 978-1-4169-9059-8 (pbk)
ISBN 978-1-4424-0944-6 (eBook)

encore pour René de mon coeur

contents

Lucky for Good

1. enemies

The enemies invaded the trailers. Many crept in alone; others arrived in organized platoons. They concealed themselves and built secret tiny nests and lairs. Some of them bit, stung, and pinched; others clogged, soiled, smudged, and polluted.

Lucky's mom, Brigitte, faced these foes like a general in World War III. She mopped, swept, vacuumed, scoured, scrubbed, washed, polished, and sterilized. She was okay with the work. It was just part of living in the little desert town of Hard Pan, Pop. 43, which Brigitte had adopted as her home when she adopted Lucky as her daughter.

Lucky herself had a live-and-let-live attitude toward Brigitte's enemies, those mice, ants, flying ants, tarantula hawk wasps, scorpions, beetles, crickets, spiders, flies, and moths, plus sand, dust, dirt, grit, and dog hair. The creatures were all just doing their jobs, trying to eat and not get eaten, make a home, have children, live their urgent tiny lives. Lucky tried to help Brigitte see things from their point of view, but it was no use. Brigitte did not care one bit about the point of view of a bug.

So Lucky was pretty conscientious about keeping the screen door closed and not tracking in dirt. She wiped down the tables on weekends, when Brigitte's Hard Pan Café was open for lunch, and she bused and washed dirty dishes. But the problem with bugs is that they don't care if a certain area "belongs" to you, like a shelf in your bedroom or a corner under the sink; all they know is, it seems like a good place to settle down. So Lucky had to be vigilant and keep up her guard, hunting and capturing the larger insects and releasing them outside.

She did her best. But sometimes all that cleaning and enemy-fighting wore Lucky out. It made her wish she were back at her old job at the Found Object Wind Chime Museum and Visitor Center, which she'd given up because of having too much else to do. For that job, she just kept the patio clean and raked; she didn't have to worry about dust or insects.

And then a certain realization bonked Lucky over the head: Nothing *stays* clean. Sooner or later the thing will have to be cleaned again. The floor, the stove, tables, pots, forks, napkins, feet, paws—the never-endingness of cleaning made a quick little what-if thought spring into her mind. The what-if was like an online pop-up, which you're forced to look at even if you don't want to. It wasn't a wish that she hoped would come true, but still, there it was, blinking at her from the corner of the screen in her mind.

It was this: What if, for some reason, Brigitte's Hard Pan Café just—*poof*—disappeared? Well, life would be way different. There would be so much less work! Brigitte could get a regular job. And they would have weekends just for themselves, to do fun things instead of working.

But then Lucky reminded herself of the good parts. Like that Brigitte wasn't homesick for France, because here in California she had a strict boss—but it was herself. And every day when Lucky got back from school, she was greeted twice: first with a dog-kiss from HMS Beagle, who was waiting at the bus drop-off, and then with a hug and a mom-kiss from Brigitte. Plus, Lucky was proud that Brigitte's cooking was famous for miles around, and all on their own, they were making the Café a success. Tourists who found them told their friends, and local people from Sierra City and other towns started coming every single weekend. It was a kind of miracle, and Brigitte said it could never have happened without Lucky. So Lucky felt ashamed about what-iffing the Café's disappearance, even for a second. She put on her yellow rubber gloves and got to work.

But then a new enemy appeared, and started a different kind of battle.

3

2. a clipboard

At first Lucky thought it was just another hungry person, the man who pulled up in a truck with **INYO CO. HEALTH DEPT. STATE OF CA** stenciled on its door.

4

"Early customer," Lucky joked, it being Friday afternoon and the Café not open until tomorrow noon. She watched from inside the kitchen trailer as the man stood by his truck, looking at the tables and at the A-frame sign:

Brigitte's Hard Pan Café
Open for
Lunch/Déjeuner
Sat—Sun & Holidays

"*Non,*" said Brigitte, also peering out the high window. "This man has a clipboard, and that is never good."

Bending down to use the toaster as a mirror, Brigitte

applied lipstick and checked her hair before stepping into the open doorway.

"Afternoon, ma'am," the man said, reaching down flat-fingered to let HMS Beagle scent his hand. He eyed Brigitte from under the bill of his cap, looking suddenly less official and more like a big clumsy friendly bear, but not sure as to the correct etiquette and wanting to make a good impression. Lucky, unnoticed, smiled to herself. Brigitte often made that impression on people, even in her thrift store hospital scrubs, her hair in a hasty ponytail: They wanted her to like them. The man held his clipboard partially behind his leg, like when Lucky's friend Miles tried to hide a stolen cookie.

Brigitte smiled brilliantly at him and then looked apologetic. "We are not open today," she said, glancing meaningfully at the sign, "but maybe you return tomorrow for lunch?"

The man removed his cap, then didn't seem to know what to do with it. He put it back on his head, the bill a little lower, as if to look more serious. When he raised the clipboard, Lucky knew he was only pretending to read it. She crossed her arms and brought one bare foot up to rest on the opposite calf of her jeans. She wanted to show the man that he couldn't just drive up any time of the day or night and expect the Café to be open. And he couldn't come around and try to scare them by acting so official. Maybe Brigitte was afraid of burros and snakes, but she was totally fearless about people. This made Lucky herself feel brave. She frowned at Mr. Inyo County Health Department mightily.

He cleared his throat. "Brigitte Trimble?" he asked, his voice deep. He planted his feet apart like a cop about to make an arrest, the clipboard now in both hands like a shield.

"Lucky, please look in the drawer to the left of the stove and bring to me the red folder," Brigitte said, not taking her clear, defiant gaze off the man. "I show you my business and fictitious name permit," she said to him, "if that is what you have come to check."

"Well, okay," he agreed, as Lucky darted up the steps to the kitchen trailer. "But this is about Regulation Number 1849. I'm Stu Burping from County Health. Mind if I have a look at the kitchen?"

Brigitte did not react, but as Lucky dashed back out with the folder, she thought, *Stu Burping, who works for the county health department? Stu Burping?* She imagined telling this tidbit of information to her best friend Paloma, and the two of them actually dying from laughter overdose.

"The clerk in Independence has assured me that my papers are in order," Brigitte said, lifting her chin, "but of course you may see the kitchen. We have no vermin or bug if that is what you wonder." Lucky hoped strongly that this man hadn't found out about the time she'd accidentally left a jar of tomato worms under a café table.

Brigitte went on, "The freezer and fridge are kept always at the correct temperature." Lucky glared at the man. He would never find a cleaner kitchen, that's for sure, and Brigitte was extremely strict about following the guidelines of the online

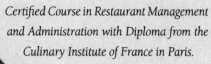

Certified Course in Restaurant Management and Administration with Diploma from the Culinary Institute of France in Paris.

Stu Burping was a little hunched, Lucky noticed, and she realized he was older than she first thought, maybe as old as fifty-five or sixty-five—anyway, in that extreme age zone where the backs of their hands and their necks are wrinkled and they get ear-hair. Grandfather age. Lucky loved the idea of grandfathers and sometimes imagined how she would have enjoyed one or two of her own. But Stu Burping wasn't here as a grandfather. She could tell from the way Brigitte had shifted to a mood where she was one-third angry, one-third insulted, and one-third just too busy. Stu Burping would not realize this about Brigitte, who seemed polite and cooperative on the surface, but Lucky read it easily in Brigitte's posture, voice, and attitude. She was not pleased.

"Pardon?" Stu Burping asked. "Kept always at what?" It was because "temperature" is written the same in French and in English, one of those words that Brigitte pronounced the French way, so with her accent it sounded like *tahmp-air-a-TURE* instead of *TEM-pra-chure*.

"The correct *temperature*," Lucky supplied.

"Oh!" Stu Burping said. "Right. TEM-pra-chure." He smiled at Lucky, then at Brigitte, who waited with a neutral expression on her face. She had been about to make a baba au rhum dessert for tomorrow, and this man was wasting her time.

"Um," he said, and used the edge of the clipboard to rub the back of his neck, papers fluttering. "Hmmm. It's more about Regulation Number 1849. No commercial cooking from a residence." He extracted two sheets of paper from the clipboard and offered them to Brigitte, who did not reach for them.

"Is your, ah, Café, operated out of your residence?" Stu Burping asked in an apologetic, only-doing-my-job voice. He smelled like V8 juice, and his brown leather shoes looked tired, as if they would rather be resting in a closet.

8

Lucky began to worry that this was a very bad situation, especially because of Brigitte's silence. It was obvious that Lucky needed to intervene. "No!" she said, trying to look as grown-up and serious and knowledgeable as possible. "Of course not! That would be a violation of Regulation Number 1849! This"—she gestured toward the kitchen trailer behind her—"is our *kitchen* trailer. Naturally we don't live there!" Lucky rolled her eyes exaggeratedly at Stu Burping to show him such an idea was ridiculous. "We *prep and cook* in the kitchen trailer, and we *live* in the other trailers that are *connected* to the kitchen trailer. So all the specimens—my dead insects and spiders and owl pellets—they're all safe in their Altoids tin boxes in my *bed*-room." Lucky gestured to her canned-ham trailer on one end and Brigitte's Westcraft at the other end. The three trailers had been soldered together in a shape like the curve of an arm, with the outdoor tables of the Café nestled in its crook.

"Lucky," Brigitte said. The way she said it meant: *Stop talking to this man immediately and let me handle it.* Lucky pretended she hadn't understood Brigitte's warning. "Come on in and look," she said, "so you can write down on your clipboard how this *kitchen* trailer is not our residence."

Brigitte took a deep breath, something between a snort and a giving-in. HMS Beagle ambled over to her side. Lucky watched Brigitte raise her eyebrows to the man, shrug, and tip her head to show he may enter. And Lucky glimpsed something else on Brigitte's face, something rare: a kind of beseeching look, a vulnerability.

This was so weird and unusual and wrong, Brigitte looking vulnerable, that Lucky felt worry churn and churn in her stomach.

Stu Burping nodded slightly, tucked his clipboard under his arm, and said, "Thank you," following her inside. Everything seemed friendly and fine on the surface, but Lucky agreed with HMS Beagle, who sniffed the ground where the man had stood and then looked, her tail low, at his truck. "I know," she told her dog softly. "What if he says we're breaking the law? What if you can get in trouble for something you didn't know was wrong? What if he ruins everything?"

But the Beag had no answer to what-ifs. So the two of them went crowding inside to find out what would happen next.

3. a cross

The official Inyo County truck had been spotted, and word of it got around town fast. On that April Saturday at noon the Café tables were loaded with customers who had heard rumors

that the county health department was going to shut down the place. Brigitte went from table to table, explaining with a laugh and a shrug that she was pretty sure Regulation Number 1849 was just a technicality, not such a terrible thing.

Lucky's friend Miles, a certified genius even though he was only six and a half (genius being one of the few things in life, Lucky had discovered, that was not age-related; you could be one even when you were a *baby*, apparently), had also heard the rumors. So Miles wanted to be there in case the sheriff came to arrest Brigitte and take her to jail. He said he would dash over to the sheriff's car and climb up onto the hood to stop them from taking Brigitte away. Lucky decided he was overreacting because his own mother had been in prison on a drug charge ever since he was very little, and she explained that whatever happened, they wouldn't actually arrest Brigitte. But Miles insisted on coming over to the Café to hang around, just to be sure; plus, he didn't want to miss any excitement, because excitement was pretty rare in Hard Pan.

Lucky watched and listened as she did table setups, noticing that the worried look on Brigitte's face from last night had been replaced by her confident smile. But Lucky also knew that Brigitte had stayed up late, reading over and over the official papers Stu Burping had left, finally slapping them down on the table and flinging her pencil against the trailer wall. From her bed, Lucky heard Brigitte go outside in the night, moving among the tables and neatly aligned chairs, her footsteps crunching on the gravelly sand in a way that had sounded sad and hopeless to Lucky.

Inside Lucky's canned-ham trailer, Miles sat on the bed, out of the way of the kitchen bustle but with the connecting door open so he could talk to Lucky as she flew in and out. He thrummed his heels soundlessly against the bed, reading *Amazing Dinosaurs* and licking celery sticks stuffed with peanut butter. Occasionally he'd peer out her porthole window, checking to see if the sheriff had arrived.

Lucky carried glasses and a half pitcher of water to table four, where two customers sat with their backs to the other tables, their helmets and leather jackets and gloves piled in a heap next to a giant Harley-Davidson. The woman, small and compact compared to her lanky, tank-topped companion, had a short, boylike haircut, with a tattoo on the back of her neck. Lucky wanted a closer look at that tattoo. They both turned as she approached, but she was able to see the design: a cross.

"Hi," Lucky said. "I'll bring the blackboard menu over in a sec."

They looked back at her and the woman squinted a little, like someone who has lost her glasses. "That's okay," she said in a high-pitched voice. "He'll have a burger with everything and I'll have a salad."

Lucky sighed and considered calling Brigitte over; let *her* explain that the Hard Pan Café didn't serve burgers like any old fast-food place; here you got something a little bit French. But she knew Brigitte was busy with a big order from table two.

Lucky poured water and decided, since she herself liked fast food, not to go into Brigitte's whole anti-burger-philosophy thing. She said, "Well, no burgers today, but we have two kinds of salads, mixed lettuce or vegetable, and some great spaghetti if you like garlic, and—wait, I'll get the board."

But the man was already unfolding himself, standing, putting a hand on the woman's shoulder. "Listen," he said to her. "I gotta go anyway. You still want to do this?"

"Yeah, I'm staying," the woman said in her high voice. "You keep in touch, okay?" She began to tap the heel of one boot rapidly against the ground, her knee jouncing up and down. "Thanks for the ride—for coming all the way out here." Turning to Lucky, she said, "A large salad—I don't care which one—and iced tea."

"Hang on," said the man, leaning over the woman. "Listen, you sure?"

The woman nodded. "Yes," she said, "positive."

He began to gather up his stuff, setting aside a plastic grocery sack bulging with something that rattled. Lucky said, "Um, by the way, there's no bus or anything here. Only the school bus to Sierra City on Monday, and they won't let you on." Lucky worried that it would turn out to be pretty inconvenient if the woman were stuck in Hard Pan, though at the same time she could hear Brigitte's voice in her head, warning her not to interfere with the customers or get into conversations where it was none of her business. Lucky *loved* to chat with the customers and always had trouble with this rule, but this time she thought it was okay.

The man was already adjusting his helmet, straddling the saddle of his motorcycle, gunning the engine loudly (which, Lucky noticed, caused Brigitte to frown). He'd fastened the second helmet to the back of his bike but left the woman's other things in a little pile in the sand.

"It's okay," the woman said to Lucky, reaching down for the grocery sack. "I'm staying here." She picked at the bag's tight knot, using her fingernails to try to tease open the plastic ties.

"*Here*? In Hard Pan? You know there's no hotel or motel or anything, right?" Lucky passed slowly beside her, hoping for a peek at whatever rattled inside that sack. She needed to find out a lot more about this woman, starting with why in the world she was staying here, and where, and who with. *And* what was in the bag. Looking down at the face frowning with concentration, Lucky was reminded of something, but she wasn't sure what—it was like getting a whiff of a smell that made you almost but not quite remember a time or a place or a person. And the harder you tried, the more the memory wouldn't let you grab it.

As the lanky guy roared off on his Harley-Davidson, the woman got the knot untied and plunged her hand into the bag. Lucky managed a quick peek inside. It was filled with walnut shells.

4. a boy named miles

In the kitchen trailer, Brigitte rapidly lined up the trays of pre-cooked vegetables and hard-boiled eggs. "We make the same salad for table four and table one," she told Lucky. "*Salade composée*, the vegetables they are all ready. Can you plate them while I make the dressing?" Lucky had watched many times as Brigitte arranged the ingredients on plates in an artistic way, quick and perfect, like food photographs in a glossy magazine, and Brigitte had explained many secret professional tips about color and texture and placement. But Lucky was not at all sure she could make the salad look so delicious and inviting.

"Pete just got here," Miles called from Lucky's bedroom trailer, where he was evidently still keeping watch at the window.

Lucky and Brigitte both smiled. Pete was a geologist who so greatly loved what he called "the crust of the Earth" around Hard Pan that he drove two hundred miles, nearly every weekend, all the way from the San Fernando Valley to their little town in the Mojave Desert.

"I bet he likes your cooking as much as he likes the crust of our Earth, Brigitte," Miles remarked.

Brigitte laughed, then rolled her eyes, then shrugged and said, "But of course he does!" And she winked at Lucky, as if they shared a little secret. Lucky smiled back, but in fact she didn't know completely what the secret was. It could have been about Miles being too young to understand complex, mature, sophisticated things, like maybe there was more involved between Pete and Brigitte than just good cooking and geology. Or about how Pete had a cool way of gazing at something most people wouldn't really notice, like a boulder, and saying, "Now *that* is dramatic." (Lucky herself considered his general constant enthusiasm quite rare and excellent, especially for a fully grown adult.)

There was a question about the wink that Lucky thought she wanted to ask, but before she could figure out what it was, Brigitte had tossed her whisk in the sink, set the dressing on the counter, and grabbed the water pitcher.

"I am taking Pete's order, Lucky. Maybe he will want the same salad, and you can just prepare one more."

"I don't think I can plate them as good as you," Lucky said.

Brigitte clicked her tongue. "Certainly you can! Not yet the dressing, but you have a sense for the color and the placement." She gave Lucky a quick one-arm hug. "Hands first, remember," she said, nodding at the sink, and then she was out the door.

Lucky washed her hands and went to work, starting with a fan of sliced mushrooms in the center of the plates, wondering what the walnut-shell woman was doing way out here in Hard Pan.

Miles came into the kitchen waving a drawing of a fierce-looking T. rex beside a chart with lots of dinosaur names neatly printed on it. "Look at this—it's a tree of life for Tyrannosauridae," he said. "They're all extinct now, but I really wish we could clone one. Or a couple of them so they could have a baby." Miles found the idea of this so funny that he snorted with laughter. "A baby tyrannosaurus! It would be as big as this trailer!"

"Very cool, Miles," she said. "Cloning's a good project for you when you grow up. Listen, I have to do these salads right now. I'll meet you in the canned ham when I get time."

"I'm a T. rex," Miles answered, and clumped heavy-footed toward Lucky's bedroom, his hands chest-high and clawed, his head swaying back and forth in search of prey, full of tyrannosaurus teeth.

"This is good, Lucky," Brigitte said after she checked each plate carefully and drizzled dressing over the salads. "It will put the customers in appetite even if they are not yet hungry. Can you do one more for Pete?" And Lucky did, full of confidence, practically an *expert* on the art of plating.

The woman smiled at the salad, and then looked at Brigitte with large dark brown eyes. "Have you heard the good news?" she asked.

Lucky wondered if this news had something to do with the motorcycle guy's departure. She collected his unused napkin and silverware as Brigitte said, "*Non*, we are busy right now"—she indicated the other customers with a sweep of her chin—"do you need anything else?"

"Only a minute of your time. Do you go to a church somewhere?"

Brigitte made her not-sure-I-understand-your-meaning face. "There is not a church in Hard Pan, but many in Sierra City—about fifty miles back to the main highway." A customer waved to catch Brigitte's eye and called, "When you have a minute!" Brigitte nodded at him, smiled at table four, and was gone.

Lucky couldn't stop staring at the woman, who seemed jittery. She still tapped the heel of one boot, and now she stuck a hand back in the bag of walnut shells on her lap, feeling around with a great deal of rattling until she brought out a small red pocket notebook. "I'll go get your iced tea," Lucky said, but she hesitated, watching as the woman fanned the notebook pages with her thumb. Despite the big rugged boots and short, chopped-off haircut, she looked delicate and feminine, and there was something familiar about her face, especially her eyes. She asked Lucky, "So, do you know all the kids in Hard Pan?"

"Yeah, there's only three of us—"

"A boy named Miles?"

When she said that, looking up with a tender smile, realization flew into Lucky's mind with the exact precision of a cactus wren landing on a yucca branch without ever being stuck by the plant's needle-sharp spines. "Hang on a sec," Lucky said, and raced to her canned-ham trailer, flinging open the door.

Miles looked up from his tyrannosaurus Tree of Life diagram. "Dinosaurs survived for one hundred sixty-five million years," he said. "They lived on the Earth much longer than *Homo sapiens* has. Even longer than—"

"Miles," Lucky interrupted, her eyes wide. "Listen! There's a lady outside at table four who asked me if I knew a boy named Miles."

Miles's open, trusting face grew flushed. Sitting very still, he said, "Who is she?"

Lucky grabbed his hands. "It's your mom!" she said. "I'm sure it's her. It *must* be Justine—she looks like you." Lucky waited for Miles to act like a firecracker with its fuse lit.

Instead he jerked his hands out of hers and turned back to his diagram, flicking a corner with his thumbnail. "No," he said. "They told us her release date isn't for another two weeks, so it's probably not her. Besides, she's not supposed to just show up like that; she's supposed to call my grandma first. What's she doing?"

"Eating a salad and asking about 'a boy named Miles'! Come on! Aren't you going out to see her?" Lucky couldn't understand why, after all this time of waiting for his mom to finish being in prison and come home, Miles was just sitting there.

He folded his diagram, creased the paper forcefully, folded

and creased it again. "What if it's not her? Or what if she doesn't recognize me?" He went over to stand by Lucky's porthole window, but he didn't look out. "Which one is table four?" he whispered, even though no one outside could have heard.

Lucky groaned and crowded beside him. He could be so stubborn! "Check it out," she said, and then drew back to give him room. "It's the one with a person staring back at us right now." Miles pressed his face to the window, unmoving, as if he were watching a very suspenseful movie of his own life.

Lucky put her arm around his shoulders. She said, "Look, I'll take you to her and I'll be right beside you."

He shrugged her arm off. "No," he said. "I can't."

She sighed, ran for the iced-tea pitcher in the kitchen trailer, and rushed back outside.

The woman who asked about Miles continued eating her salad and flicking her eyes up at the three connected trailers. She took small bites and ate quickly, like a bird. Lucky was too busy to keep watching constantly, but she did notice when the woman suddenly stood up and made her way with short, quick steps to the kitchen trailer door and knocked. "Go in, and to the left," Brigitte called to her. Customers often went inside to use the restroom.

Wanting to beam a message to Miles, Lucky stared at her porthole window. It was darker inside, so you couldn't really see in, but she radiated an urgent telepathic bulletin to him anyway.

She's coming! She's coming in to find you! It was unbearable not knowing what was going on inside, so as soon as she could, Lucky piled a tray with table three's empty dessert plates and followed the woman she was sure was Justine.

There are certain primates Lucky had seen on TV, where the young offspring clings to the mother so tightly that no matter how high she swings on the tree, no matter how fast she runs, her child stays put. This is what Lucky was reminded of when she went inside and saw the young woman standing in the middle of the kitchen with Miles in her arms. He'd wrapped his arms around her neck and his legs around her waist, clinging while she swiveled slowly from side to side, tilting back a bit to balance his weight. Their eyes were red, and both of their noses were running.

Lucky knew it was a very private moment—she knew she shouldn't stare—but she was also filled with a kind of inner triumph, as if this whole reunion was thanks to *her*. She almost couldn't bear how huge it was, this actual second; it made her a little light-headed and shaky. She dumped her plates in the washtub and ran cold water over her hands for a few minutes. She cleared her throat.

"Well," she said at last, but then didn't know

how to go on. Normal conversation was not possible. "Well," she said again, "we have homemade lemon sorbet and choco-late chip cookies for dessert." Those were the words that came out, but her voice made it sound more like *This, right now, is the incredible moment that Miles has been waiting his whole life for!* She cleared her throat and got her voice less squeally and continued, "Um, so, do you guys want some?"

Justine smiled and shifted Miles; he seemed too heavy for her. But Miles, the cookie-maniac of the world, shook his head into the curve of his mother's neck. Then he looked at Lucky with big round orangutan eyes.

Lucky saw that he wasn't about to let go, not even for a cookie.

5. triple T

Lucky's father's name was Taggart Theodore Trimble, so Lucky called him Triple T. Not to his face—she never talked to him—only in her mind, when she thought about the subject of parents. Someone can *father* a child, but that doesn't automatically make him a dad; you have to *earn* the title of dad by raising your child and by loving your child. You can't just have a baby and look at your watch and say, "Well, that's it for me! I'm out of here," and then go away forever. That's what Triple T had done, so he was her father but he was not her dad.

Lucky had never lived with him, and she only knew a few tiny things about him. This is what she knew:

He lived in San Francisco.

He was not only her birth mother, Lucille's, ex-husband; before that he had also been Brigitte's ex-husband. So Brigitte and Lucky already had the same last name, Trimble, even before they adopted each other.

Every month his bank sent money electronically to Brigitte's bank to help pay for Lucky's support.

He was a translator specializing in technical and legal papers. She thought it was strange: He spent his whole life helping people to communicate with one another, but he wouldn't talk to her.

And here is what made Lucky think she would never forgive him, even if he were sick and suffering and friendless and poor and dying: He'd never given her his address or his phone number or e-mail. The one time she'd met him, during the days after Lucille died, he had worn dark mirrored glasses so she couldn't see what he really looked like. And he hadn't even told her he was her father! He'd handed her the urn filled with her mother's ashes and he did not hug her and he let her think he was the crematory man!

He never sent anything, not even a digital card, not even a wish, on her birthday.

Except for her being born, something that he had caused to happen, certainly nothing *she* could be blamed for, she had never done anything to make him treat her like you would treat a person you hated.

In the little movies that Lucky would play in her mind, her father was on trial for a terrible crime. Lucky was called to the witness stand and swore to tell the truth, the whole truth, and nothing but the truth. Her father's lawyer tried to trick Lucky, to confuse her, and to make her look bad in front of the judge and the jury. But Lucky was filled to the brim with truth, and it made her skin shimmer and radiate light, it threw sparks from her eyes, and it enabled her to levitate, so that the lawyer had to lean back and lift his chin toward the high ceiling in order to look her in the eyes.

And the first thing she did, when the lawyer asked if she could even identify the accused, smirking because he believed she could not, was to swoop down from the witness stand, moving effortlessly and swiftly with a little buzzing sound like a dragonfly, yank the dark mirrored glasses off her father's face, and park them like a black plastic crown on top of her own head. Before anyone had time to react beyond gasps of surprise, Lucky returned to the witness chair, the question answered, the power of the glasses transferred to herself, the blinding truth acting as a force field so that no one could touch her.

In the mind movie, Lucky saw the jurors murmuring, nodding, smiling at her, the judge looking surprised and impressed that such raw power could be possessed by a mere girl, the lawyer frowning over his notes, shaking his head, at a loss. And her father bent over the table, his head on his arms, his shoulders caved in, unable to go on, defeated.

Lucky levitated over to the judge, who handed her the gavel. Everyone realized she was now both the witness and the judge. She pounded the gavel on her father's table, hard. The courtroom was silent, the jurors, judge, lawyers, bailiff, court reporter, and spectators all holding their breaths. He looked up at her, his eyes full of shame and regret.

Lucky nodded; it was a look she'd waited her whole life to see. She reached for the sunglasses on top of her head, threw them on the floor, stamped on them with her special steel-reinforced shoes.

"Guilty," she said, and glided out into the sunshine, where she was suddenly alone, and she knew that the trial was over, but she hadn't really won.

6. courage

The patio in front of the Found Object Wind Chime Museum and Visitor Center was crowded with old metal folding chairs and portable lawn chairs. Short Sammy, who was Lucky's confidant—meaning they discussed many philosophical issues—contributed his wooden packing crate. This was the crate that his outdoor bathtub, situated near the entrance of his water tank house, had arrived in. The crate was on loan as additional seating for the occasion of a town meeting, and Sammy, in stained white cowboy hat, boots, and snap-front shirt from the boys' department, was masterminding the seating arrangements.

Most everyone was there, including the newest resident, Justine Prender, milling around and sipping homemade lemonade or sun tea out of jam jars. HMS Beagle and two other dogs lay in the shade beside the museum, and Short Sammy's small dog, Roy, meandered in and out of the jumble of people as if to welcome them one by one. Since Sammy was the volunteer docent for the museum, he and Roy hung out there a lot, and Roy considered it his responsibility to make contact with each visitor.

It seemed that everyone, including the dogs, knew it was an important meeting. Ladling lemonade, Lucky and her best friend in Hard Pan, Lincoln Kennedy, waited anxiously for people to settle down and for things to get started.

Finally the Captain stood up and cleared his throat. He was the postmaster of Hard Pan, which was the only official steady job with benefits, and he usually ran the town meetings—not because he was a retired airplane pilot but because he had the commanding voice of a TV airplane pilot. Everyone settled down: Dot the beautician finished lining up two wash-and-set hair appointments, Roy found the perfect-size patch of shade, and Justine broke off in the middle of explaining to her mother, Mrs. Prender, how dental floss could be used for many things besides flossing.

"Okay," the Captain said, "we all know the county's going to close Brigitte's Hard Pan Café. For the record, the regulation is Number 1849, and Brigitte is in indisputable violation. The three connected trailers are considered their residence, and you cannot serve food commercially out of a residence in California."

Brigitte sprang up from her chair near the Captain, like a boxer before the first round. "No one tells me about this rule!" she cried. "They give me the permit for my business license but they do not mention that part. Everything about the Café is in perfect order." She stood there trembling in her pale green cotton thrift-store scrubs—slender and blazing. Lucky had seen and heard Brigitte cry several times, but realized she would never show that soft side of herself in public.

"No one here disputes that the Café is in order and that you maintain the highest standards of food preparation, Brigitte," the Captain said in his airline pilot way. Lucky was sure that every passenger on the Captain's flights had been reassured by the authority in his voice, and the same should have happened with Brigitte. But Brigitte was not reassured.

"We must close the Café," she said, "because I have not another kitchen and we have not another place to live. So we must leave Hard Pan."

Brigitte and Lucky had already discussed this, sitting at the Formica table in the kitchen trailer. Lucky hated the idea of moving. She did not like it when your whole world had to change. She had explained to Brigitte that it would break her heart and make part of her curl up and die if they had to move. Brigitte laughed, but she had tears in her eyes at the same time. She said she hoped that by selling the trailers and the land, with its beautiful view of the Mojave Desert's backyard, which is as big as an ocean, they would have enough money for a new start. Brigitte pressed foreheads with Lucky and said that as long as the two of them and HMS Beagle were together, they would be fine. Lucky had agreed with that, but she hoped with all her might that they could go on being fine together in Hard Pan.

Dot, owner of Dot's Baubles 'n' Beauty Salon, spoke up next. She had a firm, resounding voice and a firm, cauliflower-looking hairdo that resembled the hairdos of most of the other old ladies in Hard Pan. That was because they all got their wash, rinse, set, and air-dry on Dot's back-porch beauty salon, and Dot only did the one cauliflower-type style. She permed Lucky's hair too, but since it was longer, it looked more like a garden hedge. "Gonna be tough," Dot said, "to find an apartment where they'll take a good-sized dog like the Beag."

Brigitte nodded and shrugged; they would look until they found one. But this new possibility, this threat of not being able to keep HMS Beagle, weighed more than all Lucky's other worries put together. It was almost more than she could bear.

"Can't call it Brigitte's Hard Pan Café, then," Mrs. Prender proclaimed. "Won't be in Hard Pan."

"She could, too," came another voice. "She can name her Café anything she wants, irregardless where it is; there ain't no law about that. But it'd be better if the Hard Pan Café was *in* Hard Pan. Makes more sense."

"Darn shame for the town," someone added from the back. Everyone loved Brigitte's cooking and the feeling you got that you were in a little part of France when you had a meal at her Café.

Brigitte sat back down between Lucky and Pete the geologist, who now got to his feet. "It's a shame for all of us," he said. "Hard Panners, folks from Dale and Sierra City down the highway, visitors like me and the other geologists, tourists going to Death Valley, and of course the Trimbles. I think we should find a way around this."

"Let's pray," Justine suggested. She sat up very straight, reminding Lucky of the expression, "She's small for her age," as if Justine was a girl instead of a woman. Ever since she'd shown up at the Café, Lucky had secretly studied Justine. She could barely remember her from before she moved to L.A. and got herself into all kinds of trouble. So Lucky wasn't sure if the way Justine looked—so determined and fierce—had always been there, or if it was because of her time in prison. Had she already been that kind of constantly brave person—like she was used to people messing with her and figured someone was bound to do it again? Lucky didn't know, but she wished she were like Justine in that way: She wished she were brave.

"You pray, man, if you want to. But what we need is a plan." Short Sammy believed, and had made it clear to everyone, that your religion and his religion are nobody's business.

The Captain cleared his throat as Justine said to Sammy, "He counts the number of the stars; He calls them all by their names." She held up her Bible. "Psalms 147, verse 4."

Lucky found this to be a beautiful quotation, and she wanted to think about it. The words made God sound wonderfully scientific and organized, counting and naming. But she wasn't sure what it had to do with the problem of Regulation Number 1849.

Justine lifted her chin. "God pays attention to the details," she explained, as if answering Lucky's thoughts.

"Let's get back to the Café," the Captain intervened as several people began discussing Justine's comments.

Short Sammy spoke up. "Why couldn't we build Brigitte a separate kitchen right there next to the trailers? Everyone has some scrap lumber, man, and we could all pitch in with the labor."

The Captain shook his head. "I see more code violation problems with that," he said. "You know the county's going to be all over this if we come up with a new building. Sewer, plumbing, electrical, you name it. Take us months, a year, and no one here's getting any younger. Plus, the permit would cost a bundle."

"I'd help every weekend unless I have to work," Pete said.

"You got a contractor's license?"

Pete shook his head. He sat, looking defeated.

Lucky felt defeated too, and not in the least bit brave. It would be hard to move to a new town: a strange school, an apartment, starting all over with another café. No Lincoln, no Miles, no Short Sammy. It was like if one of your internal organs that you never think about suddenly stopped working. Then you would get sick and maybe even die. Hard Pan was like that—like an organ of her body that she needed in order to stay alive.

Perched on a rickety folding metal chair on Lucky's other side, Lincoln worked on a noose knot. Nooses were his latest interest, and he had explained to Lucky that the optimum number of wrappings for a hangman's noose is supposed to be eight, but that between one-half and one and a half wrappings tend to be lost during the tightening process, so you really need to make nine windings to be sure your noose will hold. "The noose," he said, "is designed to hold without slipping open when in use, while being loose enough that the hangman can slide it open to get it over the head of the person before closing it"—he raised his eyebrows meaningfully—"for the last time."

Lucky did not roll her eyes at him for going on and on about excruciating noose details because she had learned to take Lincoln's knot-tying seriously after he and his knots saved her life. She had gotten trapped in an abandoned well, and he had lowered a hammock for Lucky to get into, and then hauled her up like a fish in a net. "You know what," he said to her, "this meeting is making me wish I wasn't leaving for England in two months. I should be here to help."

Lincoln had begun tying knots when he was Miles's age, around six and a half, and recently he had won a contest given by the International Guild of Knot Tyers. His winning entry was the very hammock he'd used for rescuing Lucky from certain death at the bottom of the well. And the prize was a ticket to the annual convention of the IGKT in England during the summer, and he'd be staying with the family of the most famous knot tyer in the world, Geoffrey Budworth.

Before, Lucky had hated the idea of Lincoln going away, and she'd tried to sabotage his entry in the contest by slashing the project that later saved her life. But now, thanks to her other best friend, Paloma, Lucky was glad for him and knew she would survive his being gone. Even though Paloma lived in the San Fernando Valley, which was a three-hour car trip from Hard Pan, she visited often on weekends.

"No, England is your destiny," Lucky said dramatically. "Somehow, we'll get through this." She sighed tremendously, so that he would see that she *did* want him to go, but that at the same time, there would be unspeakable agony in her heart.

Just then a truck pulled over the ridge of the hill and chugged down into town. Everyone turned to watch, wondering who it would be, and as it came closer, Lucky knew. It was still too far away to read the words on the side, but she recognized the logo by its shape.

"It's the inspector from the county," she said. "Stu Burping."

7. just say *oui*

"Oh, man," Short Sammy said. "Who invited him?"

"Yeah, this meeting is none of his business," Henrietta growled. She'd worked in the Inyo County government office before she retired, and mostly her job for forty years had been to attend meetings, which gave her a terrible opinion of them. All those meetings had made her temperamental and argumentative. For this reason she usually avoided Hard Pan town meetings. That suited the others, because when she did show up she insisted that everybody observe official meeting guidelines that are in a book called *Robert's Rules of Order*—and Hard Panners in general disliked *any* official guidelines. But Lucky guessed that today she'd attended because she was a staunch supporter of Brigitte's Hard Pan Café, where she enjoyed sitting alone at a small table, drinking coffee, eating spicy lamb sausages, and not being in a meeting.

"I invited him," said Sass Ken, Klincke Ken's ex, who lived

about fifteen miles away, in Dale. She spoke defiantly, with a hard look on her face, like someone who expects opposition and won't back down.

Everyone looked at her in surprise, and Henrietta seemed on the verge of quoting from her battered copy of *Robert's Rules of Order* or lecturing on parliamentary procedure.

"Hold on," the Captain said. "Why, Sass?"

"Because," Sass said. "Like everyone here, I want Brigitte's Hard Pan Café to stay open. Stu Burping works for us—we pay his salary with our taxes. He should help us. And anyway, I heard he's a decent guy."

"Oh, man," Short Sammy repeated, pulling the brim of his hat low over his eyes, shaking his head. Lucky could see it was going to be like most of the town meetings, with a whole mess of different opinions and a lot of discussion, but this time everything mattered more. Because this time the meeting was about their future, hers and Brigitte's and HMS Beagle's; it was about what would become of them.

People began to murmur again; no one seemed to have any further ideas worth proposing. Then Dot stood up. She had begun using a cane recently, just to help with her balance, and now she leaned on it. "I got an old cabin," she said, "up by the mine. Belonged to my grandfather." She meant the Silverlode up on the hill, the mine that had made Hard Pan a booming town, bigger than Los Angeles was, back in the 1870s. Now the mine and all the buildings around it were shut down, fenced, and off-limits. "It's solid, good oak planks, well-built. Well, I don't need it, and can't live in it because it's on the mining company's land, or sell it except to the company, and there's no reason they would want it. So it's yours, Brigitte, if you can use it."

No one responded to this, since it didn't seem to apply to the problem, and certainly didn't solve it.

Finally Miles said, "It's too far from the Café, Dot! Brigitte can't go up there to cook and then haul the food down. It's a *restaurant*. That wouldn't work at all."

"I know that," Dot snapped. "What I'm saying is, bring that cabin down. It's small, but it would make a good-size kitchen. Set it up next to the trailers, plug into the electrical and plumbing she's already got."

"What about the building code? We're back to the idea of a new kitchen and problems of code violations," the Captain said.

Short Sammy jumped up. "The grandfather clause," he said.

Lucky felt Brigitte sigh deeply. She knew her mother was thinking that, as often happened, the meeting was in danger of veering off in some strange and unexpected direction. Why in the world was Sammy yelling about grandfathers?

"Can we please stay on track here?" someone called out from the back.

"This is on track," Short Sammy explained. "That shed Klincke Ken fixed last year, the one he uses to store things in—if I remember right, the inspector said it didn't have to come up to the same codes as for new buildings because it was already an existing structure. They call it a grandfather clause."

Lucky was trying to follow this. "Wait," she said. "First, how do you move a whole cabin? Wouldn't you have to take it all apart?"

"Naw," Klincke Ken said, holding his hand in front so he could grin without people seeing he didn't have many teeth. He was the guy everyone went to after they had worked all weekend trying to fix something, but couldn't. Klincke Ken, in exchange for a homemade pie or a six-pack of Bud Light or a tool of some kind, would always eventually find a way to make whatever it was work. "You jack it up and then lower it onto something that'll support the structure. Something like a row of old telephone poles laid horizontally. Drive a dolly under it, then tow it down the hill and over to the Café."

"What dolly?" Henrietta asked. "I never seen any dolly around here big enough to move a house on."

"Have to think about how to do it, but basically axles and wheels at the rear. I could make the dolly. That old Caterpillar loader and the lowboy trailer out near the dump still have a lot of good parts I could use."

Lucky saw Short Sammy frown, then look at Pete, who was smiling and nodding. Then Sammy also nodded. "You could," he agreed, "with a bunch of guys. Big job. But you could do it, man."

Lucky leaned sideways into Brigitte, who suddenly had tears in her eyes. *"Oh, la-la, la-la, la-la, la-la,"* she said. "It is an ingenious idea, and Dot, so generous, and Klincke Ken and

Sammy and Pete also. Thank you all. But it is such a risky plan and so much work for everyone and we do not even know if it will succeed. Also I have not the money to pay for it." She shook her head and said, in that firm way of hers that really meant it, "*Non.*"

"Hey, we don't want you to pay us," someone called. "We want you to cook for us! We'll all pitch in and help with the cabin."

Dot said, "Brigitte, listen to us. Just say *oui*!"

Sass and Henrietta began chanting, "Say *oui*, say *oui*, say *oui*!"

Brigitte got that look on her face Lucky had seen only a couple of times before, where she seemed anxious and not at all confident. Lucky figured it was because there were a lot of ways the plan might not work. Maybe the cabin would turn out to be just a shack or maybe Klincke Ken wouldn't be able to build a dolly and a tow truck out of old parts or maybe the others wouldn't help after all. If Brigitte said yes, she would have to be brave in a way of trusting everyone. Lucky tapped the side of her mother's leg with her knuckles, like someone knocking lightly at a window so the people inside would look up and notice you smiling in at them. She said, "They want you to cook for them, Brigitte."

Brigitte's cheeks flushed. "They do," she agreed. After a moment she nodded. "Okay! Lucky, you agree, yes? We say *oui*?"

Lucky hugged Brigitte hard. "Yes! We say *oui*!"

So everyone was cheering and starting to make cabin-moving plans when Stu Burping pulled up, jumped out of the truck, and waved his clipboard in the air. "I'm here to help," he said. "Name's Stu, and that's my nephew Ollie in the front seat. I guess you know I'm from County Health. Believe me, we'd rather not shut down the Café at all, but I have to enforce the code." He waved his arms over his head when everyone started talking again. "However, we don't have to close the doors right away—there's about a month leeway. So if you have any questions or ideas you want to run by me, that's why I'm here."

Lucky could tell that no one knew what to make of this—it was so strange for the enemy to do something completely unexpected and *nice*.

Pretty soon Stu Burping was shaking hands and passing out his business card, and Short Sammy was saying maybe that nephew would like to get out of the truck, have some lemonade. Lucky heard the health inspector sigh, saw him shake his head. "Oh, Ollie's going through a rough patch, and you can't blame him. His dad got laid off and can't find work—looks like their home may be foreclosed. I'm trying to get the kid out of the house once in a while, let him ride along when I do fieldwork, but he's pretty convinced the whole world's crashing down on him. It's a battle. Best, I guess, to leave him be . . ."

The Captain struggled to get everyone to come to order as voices rose. Lucky moved back to where she was partially screened by a group of people, and then she checked out the boy in Stu Burping's truck, his arms crossed, his face in a scowl.

He had that junior high way of seeming like he was too cool to
smile. She watched him watching the meeting, and that made
her see it through his narrowed eyes: the hodge-podge of folks
all talking at once about violations and God and a cabin with
a grandfather clause; and Lincoln explaining to Henrietta that
a noose is like a loop, which is a structure that can be used for
many useful things. Dogs and a cat or two wandering around,
people seated on folding chairs and stumps and old boxes
outside—there being no building in Hard Pan big enough for
everyone. And she felt a hot stab of shame that this boy—she
searched for the word to describe him: arrogant!—that this
arrogant boy was looking down his nose at her town, her *home*,
just when it seemed to be in such a hopeless mess.

41

8. depending on your point of view

Lucky wasn't sure which way it happened. Either Klincke Ken adopted the old burro who had wandered into town one day, or Chesterfield the burro came to Hard Pan and went around checking everyone out until he found Klincke Ken, and then the burro adopted the man. It all depended on your point of view.

But even after they adopted each other, Chesterfield kept wandering around, making himself unpopular by sampling flower and vegetable gardens, and people blamed Klincke Ken because now it was *his* burro. So Lucky and Lincoln went over to help him with a special project. He had to take time off his dolly-and-tow-truck-building work for moving Dot's cabin down to the Café, because this new Chesterfield-related enterprise was urgent. It was to put up a fence, made of salvaged old metal bedsprings, all around his property.

People always said Klincke Ken, never just Klincke

(pronounced Clinky) or just Ken, which was his last name even though it sounded like his first name. He'd worked as a handyman/carpenter until his back went out and he had to go on disability, though it was known that Klincke Ken could still fix anything, and if he didn't have the right tool for the job he could make one.

The burro was so tame he probably had once lived with people, although by the shaggy, rough state of his coat and the jutting-outness of his ribs, everyone agreed he'd certainly lived in the wild before moving to Hard Pan. But he'd gotten old, and Lucky figured that when he came upon the town he stopped a moment and then his tired legs didn't want to keep on. He was probably worn out from having to find his food and water on his own. She knew, of course, that burros would have no con- cept of "retirement home" or "assisted living," which is a more scrutinizing type of place where old human wrinklies live so they can take it easy and get reminded when it's time for their pills. He didn't know it, but that was exactly what this burro found.

Klincke Ken told the story as they all trooped out back to his storage shed for the bedsprings. "I'd gone out to the dump to see if there was anything to salvage, same as always on a Tuesday. Left the door open so Kirby could go in or out; that cat's got a nice temper if I ever forget *that*."

Lincoln laughed. "Cats rule," he said.

"HMS Beagle *loves* Kirby," Lucky put in. She looked back

43

toward the house, where she could see the Beag spread out on the porch and the little ginger mouser apparently massaging the dog's belly.

"So Kirby must have invited Chesterfield inside," Klincke Ken went on, "because soon's I come back and get me a Bud Light out of the fridge, I know something's different. Could feel it in the house. So I go looking for Kirby where she mostly naps. And good thing I got me a double bed because, yep, there she is and next to her is Chesterfield, spread out on his side with his hooves sticking over the edge. 'Course he's got his head on my pillow."

Lucky was a little bit curious about whether Klincke Ken changed his pillowcase afterward, but she didn't think it would be polite to ask. And besides, deep down she guessed that he wouldn't see any reason to change it.

"Well, I couldn't throw him out after *that*," Klincke Ken continued. Lucky agreed that you couldn't kick out a nice old burro like Chesterfield and still call yourself a decent member of the human race, and she wished it had been *their* place he had chosen. But she knew Stu Burping and the county health department would have found another regulation, something like Regulation Number 8472: Burros Not Permitted Within One Hundred Feet of a Café, Including Old Burros in Need of Kindness, not that Lucky could have persuaded Brigitte to let him stay anyway.

They reached the shed. From a bucket of worn-out work

gloves, they each picked out a mismatched pair: Lucky's were much too big but nicely broken in and had no holes. The shed where Klincke Ken kept his salvaged stuff was famous: It was wonderfully organized and orderly and crammed with useful things. Peering around, Lucky saw a shelf of carefully labeled, dusty glass jars. One of them was marked STRING TOO SHORT TO HAVE ANY USE.

Short Sammy was waiting for them when they returned with the first two bedsprings. He had already sunk postholes and driven in posts all around the property, each the distance from the next of a standard bed's length. That was the most difficult part of the job, because the earth of Hard Pan is as hard as cement, which was how the town got its name. Short Sammy himself did not believe in fences, and preferred living in a former water tank rather than a usual type of house. But because

Klincke Ken had helped install Sammy's corrugated tin roof he owed him a favor, so he sank the postholes.

Shade looked as if it had been spilled on the sandy ground beneath a big Chinese elm where Short Sammy waited, and there were four seats salvaged from old VW vans, so everyone decided they should take a break before starting in on the work. Klincke Ken went inside for refreshments, returning with four canned drinks.

"You're giving that stuff to kids?" Short Sammy asked.

Klincke Ken shrugged. "Won't hurt 'em."

Lincoln picked up a can. "Ensure? What is it?" He had in his other hand a sturdy small loop he had designed like a noose from strips of braided leather—it was going to be the latch for the new gate.

"It's normally for folks like me who can't chew," Klincke Ken explained. "Stuff gives you all the vitamins and nutrients and whatnot." Lucky had noticed before that his teeth were mostly gone. If he had to smile or laugh, he covered his mouth with his hand.

Short Sammy took a swig. "It's not bad, man. A little sweet."

"I liked it at first, but now I'm sick of it," Klincke Ken confessed.

"What about getting new teeth?" Lucky asked.

Klincke Ken stared at her. Finally he said, not as a question but as a statement, "New teeth."

"You could, man," Short Sammy said.

Lucky said, "That Ensure stuff, it looks really . . . thick."

She did not think she wanted an entire can of liquid vitamins.

Lincoln, who was always hungry, took an enormous gulp. "It is," he said. "Thick and vitaminy. Must be pretty good once in a while, but I can see why you'd get hungry for regular food." Lincoln's full name was Lincoln Clinton Carter Kennedy, and he had not yet broken the news to his mom that he didn't want to grow up to be the president of the United States, as she hoped he would. But Lucky marveled, as always, at how diplomatic and presidential he just naturally was.

"What I'd miss," Short Sammy said, "would be those real thin pork chops fried in bacon fat, when they get almost crunchy."

"New teeth," Klincke Ken said again, like it was an interesting new flavor in his mouth that he'd never tasted before.

"You can even choose what color you want, man," Short Sammy said. Lucky was impressed at how much he seemed to know about false teeth. She tasted a little sip out of Lincoln's can and decided privately that the stuff was awful and resolved to do a way better job of brushing her own teeth so she wouldn't lose them when she got old.

Suddenly Klincke Ken stood up. "I want a steak," he said, "and pork chops and peanuts and apples and corn on the cob. And I want some fancy cooking. Lately it's got so I can't hardly stand how good it smells down there at Brigitte's Hard Pan Café on weekends." His face took on a fierce expression. "I'll do it," he said. "And I've got what I need out in the shed."

As he trudged back there, Lucky looked at Short Sammy

with large, wondering eyes. "He doesn't have some old false teeth that he salvaged?" she asked him.

Short Sammy laughed. "Never know, man," he said. "He can fix anything, that's been proven. And he never gives up on a project once he gets started."

Klincke Ken carried an old paint can when he re-emerged. Dried paint drips covered most of the label, but the name of the color, Grizzle White Enamel, could still be read. "Enamel," he said, "you know, the word 'enamel,' that's what reminded me of *teeth* enamel and *paint* enamel when Sammy talked about color. But I don't want anything too flashy or too white, so that if my new teeth get a little stained it won't show too much. I'm taking this empty can to give to the dentist and see if they can match this exact color."

Grizzle White Enamel was a shade or two less yellow and a bit more gray than the color of Chesterfield's big chompers, but Lucky thought that the old burro and the old man would have nicely coordinated smiles once Klincke Ken got his new teeth.

Klincke Ken put a hand to his mouth and smiled behind it. They could tell by his eyes that he was smiling. "Gonna put some of my disability money aside and have myself lunch down at the Café, regular every Sunday, once I get fixed up. I owe all this to Chesterfield and to you," he said to Lucky. "Me, I'da never thought of new teeth."

"Well," said Lincoln. "Let's get this fence put up before Chesterfield wanders off again."

So Lucky put on her worn-out gloves, the sweet taste of

Ensure at the back of her throat. The metal bedsprings were all different; they came in a variety of curlicue patterns, each of them beautiful and quite strong. In Lucky's opinion the new fence added a distinctive, unusual look to Klincke Ken's place; even Short Sammy admired it.

Dot dropped by just as they finished. She squinted at the fence and said, "Those are *bed*springs. I thought fences are supposed to be made out of wood or chain link or even chicken wire, but I never heard of one made out of junk."

"Well, Dot," Lincoln said. "From Chesterfield's point of view, because he was used to living wherever he wanted, this fence is how he knows what's home and what isn't home. It's a good fence if it keeps him out of trouble, right?"

"Sure," Dot said, because she was the kind of person who wanted to be agreeable, "I guess it's good." Then, because she was also the kind of person who wanted to have the last word, she added, "If you like bedsprings."

9. ollie martin

Nobody sat on the splintery unroofed official bus-stop bench in front of Sierra City Elementary. Instead the Hard Pan kids and the Dale kids waited for Sandi the bus driver on a low, wide concrete wall nearby. It was a handy, convenient wall for hanging around on—you could straddle it, face-to-face with another person, to have a private conversation, or you could lie on it and gaze up into the leafy ceiling of a cottonwood tree. But if you sat facing front in the normal way, like on a regular bus stop bench, you would be staring at your future: Einstein Junior High, right across the street. Everything about Einstein worried Lucky, from its name (which made you think you had to be a genius to go there) to its student population. Those students were all bigger and older and what Paloma called, in one of their many discussions of the pitfalls and dangers of junior high, way more experienced.

On that warm late April afternoon, two girls from Dale

straddled the wall knee-to-knee, playing a fast hand-clapping game; Miles organized his Old Testament trading cards; and Lucky lay on her back, reading a very good book about the love aspect of Charles Darwin's life. She hoped Lincoln would hurry up; he was discussing with Ms. Baum-Izzart a project he wanted to get school credit for during the summer in England. If the project was about nooses, Lincoln should not emphasize that aspect to the principal, in Lucky's private opinion. Nooses were just knots to Lincoln—well, as he'd explained, not *just* knots, but very special, specific knots that had to be done right the first time—but a principal would probably be creeped out about the *idea* of nooses and not understand his interest in the technical aspect. As Lucky thought about this, she noticed a boy across the street at Einstein, heading toward them. He carried a skateboard.

Lucky was surprised to see that it was the nephew who had been in Stu Burping's truck at the town meeting. When he got to the curb, he threw the skateboard down, jumped on, and spun it around. Then he leaped the curb, got up speed, reversed direction, and made the board spring up into the air, as if it were glued to his feet. The board landed on its side, so the underneath was visible; like the top, it was decorated with elaborate, colorful designs. And written on it in multicolored puffy-graffiti letters was the name OLLIE MARTIN.

"Hey, I need to practice some tricks on that wall," he called out, flipping the board up with the toe of his sneaker. "You guys clear off."

The Dale girls, who were third graders, swung their legs over and moved obediently to one side. But Miles looked up from his trading cards and said, "This is *our* school's wall."

"Well, no," Ollie Martin said with mock patience and mock friendliness. "Right now, that wall is *my* wall."

"Look," Lucky said, "the bus'll be here in a minute, and then you can have it all to yourself."

The skater rocked his board, clacking the pavement, and pulled a stick of Juicy Fruit from his pocket. "Oh, right," he said conversationally, like they were just old friends shooting the breeze, "the bus that goes"—he paused, smiled, and threw the gum wrapper on the ground—"to the *outlying areas*." He said "outlying areas" in a sarcastic way that stung Lucky, as if underneath that official teacher phrase lurked some awful meaning.

"Just Dale and Hard Pan," Miles explained.

"Oh! Just Dale and Hard Pan," the boy repeated, still with that fake niceness, as if *he* knew so much more, as if they were babies. He smacked his Juicy Fruit. It was becoming more than Lucky could bear.

She said, "So, *Ollie*, were you actually named for a skateboard trick or what?"

Ollie Martin didn't hear the little jab of irony in Lucky's voice, or if he did, he chose to ignore it. "Actually, yeah," he said. "My dad was a world-class skateboarder." Everyone stared at him; you couldn't top that for dad coolness. This annoyed Lucky further; Ollie was just plain showing off. He pulled out another stick of gum and peered down the street—no bus was coming—then made a sweeping gesture that clearly meant, *Get off the wall now.* Lucky ignored this; she turned to the next page in her book. Miles stacked his cards.

Ollie narrow-eyed Lucky, dropping the second wadded-up gum wrapper onto the ground. He flipped his board up in the air, caught it, and examined the underside as if to double-check his own name. He said, "I've been to Hard Pan. That's where some illegal immigrant got busted by the health department." He nodded, agreeing with himself. "Everyone's heard about that, because, like, the whole town is full of trailer trash and welfare losers. Same kind of people who make hardworking Americans lose their jobs." Ollie whacked the board hard against his thigh, sending the wheels spinning. "So in the loser town of Hard Pan this woman opens a restaurant, and what was that specialty on the menu?" Ollie didn't ask this as if he expected an answer. He asked, Lucky knew, because he wanted to answer it himself. "Oh, yeah, ground-up ratburgers. Just add a lotta garlic, and they say it tastes almost like chicken."

"What is *wrong* with you? Shut *up*," Lucky said, but she knew she couldn't make him, and Ollie Martin knew it too. He wore skateboard scrapes and road rash on his big-boned arms and a cooler-than-you-can-ever-hope-to-be expression on his face.

Ollie rolled his eyes, signaling he was out of patience. "Listen, children, this is wasting my time. Why don't you two go play over there with the other little girls."

Lucky blazed as if she'd been set on fire. "We are not children!" she shouted, even though they *were* children. What she really meant was, *Quit acting like you're better than us!* He gave her his little gum-smacking smile, and she yelled, "Get out of here, big red-nosed creepo!" Not a very good insult, but it was all she could think of.

"I know who you are. I saw you." Ollie moved close to Lucky, looming over her; he smelled like gum and the oil on his skateboard wheels. "You were with the ratburger lady. I heard the county got there just in time before she poisoned the whole town."

Suddenly Lucky clambered up so she was standing on the wall. Now she was taller than him. "Yeah, I was with her, and don't you dare call her that. She happens to be my mother, and she's a professional chef and she cooks better than you can even *imagine*, so back off!"

Instead of backing off, though, Ollie sneered again in his cool, horrid, junior high way, as if he'd just scored a point. "Oh, give me a break. Tell her, fine, be a professional chef, but stay in her own country instead of coming here and putting Americans out of a job. Come on, figure it out; it's not that complicated. She's working the system."

Lucky didn't know exactly what this meant, but it sounded bad and insulting. She said, "She's a naturalized American citizen!"

Ollie ignored this. He added yet another stick of gum to the wad in his mouth, flicking the crumpled wrapper toward Lucky. "So where's your father? I bet you don't have a clue."

Maybe because it was a question she could not answer or because she was sick of Ollie Martin's attitude, and sick of the way he made Hard Pan seem like a dump, and sick of how he'd attacked Brigitte without even *knowing* her, and sick of his *gum.* So, without realizing it, she drew her hand back and then rammed it forward with mighty force, punching him on the jaw. She felt the impact of it all the way to her shoulder and heard a hard thud, like a bag of wet sand dropped on the ground. Then almost immediately her arm was being yanked hard behind her. She was shoved down and pushed onto her stomach, her cheek raking the dirt.

"You little—" Ollie held her down, ramming a knee in her back. But suddenly it stopped. Ollie was off her, there was shouting, and she sucked in air, trembling uncontrollably, not sure, as she got on all fours, if her muscles would allow her to stand. Her knuckles burned as if they had skidded on concrete; her legs shook as she swayed on her hands and knees. She felt like throwing up.

And then many things were happening at once. It was hard to pay attention, hard to focus, because Lucky was filled with a powerful urge, if only she could get to her feet, to go roaring after Ollie Martin and pound him, *pummel* him with her fists. But she was scared, too, because she knew now how strong he was. And seething hot anger spurted through her veins because he was so wrong about her mother, but—and this made her more infuriated—right about her father.

And finally she was sitting on the wall, spitting out dirt, and Sandi the bus driver's voice was nearby, with the static of her two-way radio. Sandi was saying, "Ambulance at the Sierra City Elementary bus stop. A kid is hurt."

Then Lucky felt a rich gladness wash through her: It was

okay. She was apparently injured but would live, and Ollie Martin would get in deep, deep trouble for hurting her.

But when she checked herself, Lucky found out she was not the one who had been hurt, except for her feelings and her pride. It was Lincoln, propped against the wall, his face white and filled with pain, cradling his right arm to his chest.

"Get back, Miles. Move away!" Sandi shouted. "I need a clear path here."

Lucky watched as Miles picked something up off the ground, scooted out of the way, and came to sit on the gravel between her and Lincoln.

"I don't get why that boy hates us so much," he said, frowning up at Lucky. "But you shouldn't have socked him. You'll probably have to go to hell for that." He swiped the back of an arm across his eyes and glared at her.

"No, she won't," Lincoln said, his voice strained.

Lucky was still a little breathless, as if she'd almost drowned. "Oh, Miles," she said. "It'll be okay."

As the ambulance pulled up, she glanced down at Miles. Arms wrapped around legs, forehead on knees, and his lips, Lucky could see, silently moving. And clenched in one fist she saw what he had been carefully gathering up from the ground: a handful of Juicy Fruit gum wrappers. She reached over and cupped her hand underneath his; he relaxed his fingers, letting the papers fall into her palm. "What's up with this, Miles?" she asked.

"I wanted to spur that boy Ollie on, and you, too, Lucky."

"Spur us on?"

"It was really *scary*, you don't *know* how scared I was, and when he knocked you down on the ground before Lincoln came I just wanted to beat him up, but I was too scared. All I could think of was how Justine says if we're mad or scared we should do a good deed to 'spur one another on toward love.' But I don't know if picking up his trash was a good enough deed. I don't know if it worked."

Lucky looked at the crumpled wrappers in her hand and then over at Ollie, slumped against a tree with a hand to his jaw. His skateboard had been confiscated by Sandi. Without it, his limbs seemed useless and limp, as if the skateboard was an engine his body couldn't run without.

She squeezed the wrappers hard, into a tight little ball, but she was not spurred on toward love and there were no good deeds in her angry heart.

10. the principal's office

Ms. Baum-Izzart was not wearing her usual cheerful-but-businesslike look. She frowned over a form on her desk, a form, Lucky guessed, that detailed yesterday's fight at the bus stop. A framed photo of a smiling, curly-haired man holding a tiny bald newborn baby was propped on the desk, facing those who waited for the principal. It was a little weird to think of Ms. Baum-Izzart as a mom, a person with a domestic life she went home to every day, changing diapers and laughing with her curly-haired husband and making coffee. Lucky felt cheered for a moment at the thought of her having a whole private non-principal life of her own as a regular human being.

It is not comfortable or easy to sit in a principal's office, waiting for a verdict. Lincoln appeared calm and relaxed, his sprained wrist encased in a splinted black brace with Velcro closures. Lucky knew she was in trouble, and it made her squirm in her own wooden chair. Occasionally she sneaked sideways looks at the boy she had punched, the eighth grader Ollie Martin.

Lincoln was the only one not in trouble. He had arrived at the bus stop just when Ollie twisted her arm, shoved her down, and pinned her to the ground by thrusting his knee in her back. Lincoln had thrown his skinny, muscular arm around Ollie's neck from behind, pressing hard against his throat. That forced Ollie, stocky and fifteen pounds heavier, to jump off of Lucky in order to send Lincoln flying backward. Lincoln sprained his wrist when he landed and was told by the X-ray technician he was fortunate the bones hadn't fractured.

Lucky hoped and fully expected that Ollie Martin would get the brunt of the punishment, whatever it turned out to be. She still seethed at his nasty insults to Brigitte and hoped he'd be kicked out of school and sent to a military academy where he would have to wear a uniform and say "sir" to everyone and eat bad food and sleep on a metal cot. Brigitte and Ollie Martin's mom and Lincoln's parents had already come to the school for a meeting, but Brigitte would only say they all agreed to let Ms. Baum-Izzart and the junior high principal decide each of their fates.

When a tall, thin-haired man tapped on the open door, Ms. Baum-Izzart got up, shook his hand, and offered him the remaining chair. She introduced everyone briskly: He was Dr. Strictmund, the principal from Einstein Junior High. It was not the type of social situation where you're supposed to smile and say how glad you are to meet the person, so Lucky and Lincoln both just said hi, and Ollie Martin leaned forward in his chair, avoiding eye contact. Dr. Strictmund did not seem as if he would have a baby or a wife or even an interesting hobby. He looked like his one true identity was principalness, and it ruled every moment of his life. Lucky was sure that he drove his car like a principal and heated frozen spinach in the microwave like a principal and fluffed his pillow like a principal. He even smelled like a principal, starchy with a whiff of Pine-Sol.

"Okay," Ms. Baum-Izzart began. "First, all of you need to know that fighting of any kind is completely unacceptable. There is never a reason to fight, especially on the school grounds. I am very, very disappointed in you."

"I didn't plan to," Lucky blurted. "I couldn't help it. He was telling lies. He said my mother—" She broke off, unable to repeat the insult.

"He said Brigitte poisoned us," Lincoln finished, in a matter-of-fact way.

Ollie slid down in his chair, snorting. "You're all against me," he said. "It's four against one. Why don't you just suspend me and get it over with?"

"Ollie, sit up and stop that behavior," Dr. Strictmund ordered. "Throughout this session I'll be monitoring your non-verbal communication and the way you comport yourself. You are *not* running this meeting. I want to see if you are mature enough to discuss the incident now or if you would rather do litter collection every day for a week and then have the meeting."

Dr. Strictmund's eyes, the beaming laserlike eyes of a principal, bore into Ollie Martin. Lucky glanced at Lincoln, thrilled: Ollie Martin was really going to get it. Lincoln raised his eyebrows minutely: code for *wait and see*.

Ollie overcorrected his posture in a false, super-obedient way, as if he were following Dr. Strictmund's instructions, but Lucky knew that he did it sarcastically. She dreaded the time not far off, when she would be surrounded by boys in that age group.

"Moving on," Ms. Baum-Izzart said. "Lucky, you hit Ollie first. That was a choice and a decision you made. You need to take responsibility for that, and realize that you could and should have walked away or ignored him."

"Besides," Ollie Martin said, "it's a free country. I just said what everyone already knows, that they're running an illegal business and the county's shutting them down. When foreigners come here, they have to follow the rules like everyone else."

Lucky blazed with indignation but kept her mouth shut, because Dr. Strictmund beat her to it. "This is your last warning, Ollie," he barked. "What goes on among adults, and Mrs. Trimble's establishment, is none of your business."

What happened next surprised everyone, even Lucky. Maybe it was because he'd called Brigitte's Hard Pan Café "Mrs. Trimble's establishment," which made it sound sort of shady, like it was something bad. But Lincoln looked at Dr. Strictmund and said, "Sorry, sir, but I disagree."

"Lincoln," Ms. Baum-Izzart said, "our understanding is

that you broke up the fight and got a badly sprained wrist when Ollie shoved you off. Are you changing your story?"

Everyone waited for Lincoln's answer. Ollie Martin, whose body, Lucky thought, seemed too big for him to live in easily, leaned forward, elbows on knees, forehead on the heels of his hands, as if he were staring at the floor, but actually he peered sideways at Lincoln.

"What's going on with Brigitte's Hard Pan Café concerns everybody," Lincoln said, "not just the adults. It's true that there are a lot of rumors, and people jump to conclusions. Lucky was trying to set the record straight. Kids are as affected by this as much as adults, maybe more."

How did Lincoln always know what to say, and how to say the right thing at exactly the right time? Even though he was kind of letting Ollie Martin off the hook, he was also standing up to Dr. Strictmund and defending Lucky.

"Point taken," Dr. Strictmund said unexpectedly. He nodded in a certain principal-like way at Ms. Baum-Izzart.

"But," Ms. Baum-Izzart said, "we still have the issue of fighting. Lucky and Ollie, I'm waiting to hear whether or not you both take responsibility and will find ways *never* involving physical violence to resolve differences."

"Otherwise," Dr. Strictmund put in, "you'll both be suspended on the spot."

"But doesn't he"—Lucky jerked her chin at Ollie Martin—"get some kind of punishment?"

Lincoln moved the worn toe of his Converse back and

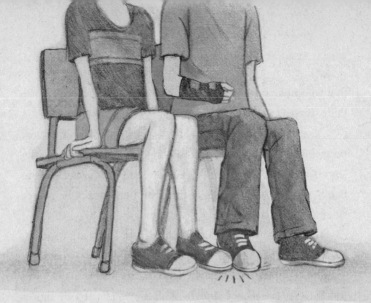

forth, a little sweeping motion that made Lucky realize, as Ms. Baum-Izzart's puckered eyebrows also signaled, that she had put her foot in her mouth.

"Um," she went on in a rush, "and *I* promise not to hit boys twice my size even when they bad-mouth my mother." Lucky saw a tiny smile flit onto her principal's face, then quickly disappear.

Dr. Strictmund nodded again. He turned his laser-beam eyes on Ollie Martin, who made a show of sitting up straight in his chair again. "Right," Ollie said. "She almost broke my jaw. But next time it happens I'll just stand there and let myself get hit. Okay?"

"I'm not really hearing a resolution here," Ms. Baum-Izzart said. "Obviously, everyone needs to work harder at finding acceptable ways to resolve conflicts. I want some *positive thinking* from you." She turned to Ollie. "Dr. Strictmund and I were especially disturbed by the aspect of prejudice in your taunting of Lucky's family," she said. "This is a country of immigrants. Do you know anything about your own heritage?"

For the first time Ollie lifted his eyes, which had astonishingly long lashes. He looked back at Ms. Baum-Izzart defiantly. "Yeah, we're white. So what?"

"Change that tone, Ollie," said Dr. Strictmund, "or this will get much worse."

Ollie muttered, "I don't see what my race has to do with anything."

"Dr. Strictmund and I think it would be a good learning experience for you to find out more about your own background. Lincoln's mother, Mrs. Kennedy, works at the Sierra City Library, and she has agreed to help you do some genealogical research. We want you to make a family tree. Start with your parents' generation. List their full names and where they were born. That's the easy part."

Ms. Baum-Izzart went on, "Then do the same with both sets of their parents, your grandparents. And we want you to go back another generation before that: names and places of birth of your great-grandparents. Mrs. Kennedy believes you'll be able to fill in some of your family background through online sources, and she'll guide you with the research.

"Lucky, your assignment is different. You need to think

more about consequences—how your actions and your decisions affect other people as well as yourself," Ms. Baum-Izzart said. Lucky frowned. This was not sounding good.

"Please think about what I just said. Then write a thousand-word report on the subject of actions and their consequences. Start with an outline and include your thoughts on—"

Lucky disliked written reports more than any other type of homework. The biggest problem was how boring they were. The boredom secretions from writing a long report, she believed, could actually harm every lobe of the brain—especially a tender young developing brain like hers. Principals did not always realize the health ramifications of the *torture* of writing one thousand words, especially on a topic such as consequences, which was seriously boring before you even got started. Instead of letting her principal continue to describe this extreme punishment, Lucky interrupted, "Wait, that's not fair! If he has to make a family tree, then I should have to make a family tree."

There was a silence. The two principals exchanged a glance. Lucky noticed this and then suddenly realized what it was about. She stood up.

"Ms. Baum-Izzart," she said slowly, "is it because I'm adopted? Is that why you don't think I can make a family tree?"

Another look between the principals confirmed Lucky's suspicion, but Ms. Baum-Izzart said, "Lucky, please sit down. It's not that we don't think you *can* make one. It's rather a situation where we assumed a family chart might be more relevant to you when you're older. Remember, Ollie is in the eighth grade;

you're in sixth. Whereas the essay would be a way for you to focus on—"

To her horror, Lucky felt tears prickling behind her eyeballs. She sat down and tilted her head back slightly to keep them, if possible, from spilling over. A mental image came to her of Miles's T. rex Tree of Life chart, which was kind of like a family tree except it showed millions of years instead of several generations. This thought made her feel calmer.

"Could I just say something?" Lucky asked. Miraculously, the tears slid back down inside her head. "My biological family is not extinct. They are my bloodline." A new idea, a way of explaining, came to her in a rush. "It's like my dog," she said. "She has a dog father and a dog mother, dog grandparents and great-grandparents, even though she doesn't know them. They're her bloodline. *And* she has an adopted family, which is me and Brigitte. Well, and Lincoln, and also Miles. And of course Short Sammy and Roy. And really Dot, too, and the Captain—"

Lucky sensed she was losing the thread. "Anyway . . ." She looked at Ms. Baum-Izzart, whom she had known since the age of five, and at Dr. Strictmund, a stranger. Both were tapping the eraser ends of their pencils, as if eraser-tapping were taught in Principal School as a technique of getting students to stay focused. "Anyway," she said again, "one *positive consequence* of my socking Ollie in the jaw would be finding out about my other family, my biological family." *Finding out about my father*, she thought, and had to tilt her head back again for a second. "It seems only fair—"

Dr. Strictmund cleared his throat loudly. He looked at Ms. Baum-Izzart. She nodded. They both quit tapping their erasers and put their pencils down. Monitoring this nonverbal communication and the way they comported themselves (probably more techniques they got from Principal School), Lucky was impressed. "Okay," Ms. Baum-Izzart said. "We see your point. I just need to be sure: Are you certain you want to do this research, Lucky?"

"Hey, how come you let *her* decide?" Ollie demanded. "If she gets to do a family tree, I should get to do an essay."

"Hold on, here. This is getting out of hand," Dr. Strictmund said.

"You *like* writing essays?" Lucky asked, turning to Ollie.

"Yes, way out of hand," Ms. Baum-Izzart agreed. "No more interrupting for any reason." (But Lucky stayed facing Ollie and big-eyed him as a way of saying, *Really?* And he eye-rolled her back as a way of saying, *Anything is better than a dorky family tree.*) Ignoring them, since at least they weren't *verbally* interrupting, Ms. Baum-Izzart continued. "All right. The assignment is to do a family tree. It will be a way for both of you"—she turned her gaze from Lucky to Ollie and back to Lucky—"to discover an aspect of who you are. It will give you something to think about besides hurting each other. Do you both understand?"

Ollie breathed out through his mouth noisily and cracked the knuckles of his left hand. He said, "Yeah, fine." Lucky figured he'd gotten off easy, whereas she had a ton of work to do, since she practically didn't know anything about her biological ancestors. A tinge of regret about what she'd gotten herself into began to seep throughout all her brain lobes.

Now she worried that she ought to have begged for a different punishment, like community service. She would much rather have done that, helping Short Sammy clear litter from his adopted highway, the two of them out in the forest of Joshua trees, the giant tortured-looking ancient ones with their dried-out twisted branches, the younger ones with fewer limbs, the green pups and babies growing like thick straight spiky-headed sticks. Then she realized the two principals' pencils were eraser-tapping again, and she felt the slightest nudge to the side of her foot, but Lincoln was gazing at Ms. Baum-Izzart's photo as if he'd touched her just by chance.

So Lucky shrugged in a Brigitte-like way, to show it didn't matter much to her anyway, and without thinking about it she repeated Ollie's exact words. "Yeah, fine," she said, and only then did the slight pressure cease, of Lincoln's shoe against hers.

Dr. Strictmund said, "Ollie, Lucky," and waited until they both looked at him. He held their eyes for a moment, the way principals do, and said, "You need to take this seriously. We want good work from you and we want it on our desks in a month. None of your other work is to fall behind." And then, with the exact tone and expression of a principal, he said, "This meeting is over."

11. a prickly tree

On a large sheet of paper, Lucky penciled a spiky Joshua tree with a trunk that divided into two branches. Those in turn split into four branches, and then into eight, pointing in all directions and covered with sharp spines. It was neither pretty nor friendly-looking, so since she was having such a prickly time trying to get close to her ancestors, Lucky considered the Joshua an ideal choice for her family tree.

The scent of simmering red wine filled the kitchen trailer—Brigitte was making a stew of chicken in wine sauce—as Lucky reflected that Ms. Baum-Izzart had been right. There *are* consequences to every action, including the very fact of having talked the principal into giving her this family tree assignment. Half of her wanted badly to fill in the names and dates of her biological family on the thistly branches, but the other half dreaded it. Because the first dismal consequence was that Lucky was going to have to ask for answers from the one person in the world she couldn't talk to. She was going to have to ask her father.

"Do you think it's educational," Lucky demanded, turning around to watch Brigitte drop a bundle of fresh herbs into the pot, "or even very *polite*, for students to have to dig and dig and dig around to find out about ancient relatives? I say it's *not*, and it's a violation of dead people's privacy, and what good is it? Zero! When you could be doing something interesting and useful, like collecting owl pellets! And what does it have to do with—"

"Wait," Brigitte said, and reminded Lucky, with a long level look, that she had heard these complaints before. She lowered the heat under the burner. "I know. The true dilemma is your father."

Lucky added more spiky thorns to her tree, pressing down hard with the pencil. It now looked to her like a cross between a porcupine and a bunch of sledgehammers. Brigitte continued, "But no matter what the dilemma, Lucky, you must do this work and you must do it correctly. You know very well that it is because you were fighting at school."

"Yes, but—"

Brigitte interrupted, "So now maybe I should not, but I tell you something new. There is an older sister, or maybe she is a half sister. She is in, perhaps, Oregon. Your father, he one day gives me her number in case there is an emergency—if he is to die. He tells me they argue long ago; for many years they are not speaking." She paused, clamped a heavy lid over the pot, and headed toward her bedroom trailer. "Even though he has not died, it is now *une urgence*, a case of urgency. I am going to give you the number of this sister."

Lucky dropped her pencil on the Joshua tree drawing and sat very still. She thought, *Another aunt!* One minute she had two French aunts, Brigitte's sisters, who were called Tante Celeste and Tante Liliane; the next minute she had a whole new aunt in Oregon, a living relative she'd never known about.

Her father had a sister! The wish to have a sister of her own sometimes gripped Lucky like hunger pangs. But her father, who *did* have one, wasn't speaking to her. Lucky would never understand him.

Brigitte returned with an old-fashioned adding machine and her small suitcase, the one she had brought to America. The suitcase always reminded Lucky of the time of sadness, when she was eight and her mother Lucille was killed by stepping on a fallen power line after a storm. Lucky's father (who did not want to take care of his only child) thought of something no one else would have dreamed up in a million years, and he called up his first wife in France. He asked her if she would come to California—he would pay for her airline ticket—to help out, just for a little while.

As Brigitte opened the suitcase, Lucky replayed in her mind the next scene of the story deliciously—she had heard it told over and over—because it was the miracle part. So that first wife, who was impulsive and loved children and had always wanted to see California, instead of hanging up on her ex-husband, listened with her heart. That's the way she told it, and it made Lucky imagine her putting the phone to her chest as if her heart had its own tiny ears to hear his words. Then, just like that, she said yes. And she turned out, of course, to be Brigitte.

Now Brigitte used the little suitcase for keeping important things, like her certificate of American citizenship and Lucky's adoption papers. She flipped through a small green worn-out book with CARNET D'ADRESSES on its cover. "I file her under Trimble because I know I will forget her married name. Here— Siobhan Kelly in Portland, Oregon. I think she has the same father as Tag, and a different mother. You need to call her, Lucky."

12. elder futhark

Lucky worried about having a conversation with this stranger-aunt. What if she was like Lucky's father, unwilling to talk? And what if she hadn't ever heard of Lucky, so that the whole complicated story of her two mothers would have to be explained? Lucky wanted more information before getting immersed in these problems.

She flipped open the Dell. "If we find her on Facebook, maybe we could get her e-mail. Then I could write her instead of talking."

"Okay, but only to search for her e-mail, Lucky," Brigitte said, and leaned over to log in to her Facebook account. Then she slid into the opposite side of the banquette, plugged in the adding machine, and reached for her folder of unpaid bills.

Lucky entered "Siobhan Kelly" in the Facebook search box, got a list of 392 possibles, and groaned. She began scrolling down, looking for a hometown of Portland. No luck. "Drat," she said to HMS Beagle, who was lying on the floor, giving her paw pads a thorough grooming.

Lucky decided to try Siobhan Trimble Kelly and was rewarded with fewer hits, and one of those listed Portland as the hometown. "I think I found her!" Lucky said.

"You cannot be sure." Brigitte leaned over and peered around at the screen. "She gives contact information, an e-mail address. I want you to get off Facebook and just send her an e-mail. Then, if she is not the right person, she will not have my full name."

"I know," Lucky said distractedly, thinking of what she could write. She copied the e-mail address, logged off Facebook, and pasted the address into her "Send To" e-mail box. She typed:

> If you are related to Tag Trimble

[Lucky decided not to say "if he is your brother" as a way of testing, later, should Siobhan Kelly reply, whether she was really her aunt and not just someone fooling around]

> then I hope you won't mind if I ask you some questions.

She signed it "A Friend You Have Never Met from the Past."

Lucky envisioned this cyber-aunt looking at her e-mail address, which was Beagle@burgoo.com. She would not know Lucky's name, or anything about her. She clicked send.

Lucky stared at her e-mail in-box. Empty. She willed a message to appear. Nothing. Well, so the maybe-aunt wasn't online. Lucky gave up and got out her social studies homework. The problem with social studies was that it took up valuable time and normally was of quite limited interest. Right now Lucky's class was studying the Vikings. The Vikings used written symbols called runes, and they had an alphabet called Futhark. Okay, this was a little bit interesting, but it wasn't *useful*, the way studying about, for instance, animal adaptation was useful. Why Ms. Grundy wanted her students to learn about Futhark was beyond Lucky.

She looked up Futhark in Wikipedia and discovered that there was an Elder Futhark and a Younger Futhark. Great.

Lucky switched to e-mail and checked her in-box. Empty.

She pressed on with Futhark. The knowledge of how to read Elder Futhark had been forgotten (this was no surprise to Lucky) for centuries. Then someone figured it out at about the time of the Civil War. Wikipedia had a chart of runes with their equivalent English alphabet letters, but when Lucky decided to write her name in Elder Futhark, she discovered the Vikings had no *C*. How weird was that? A whole language with no *C*!

Searching further, she found a website with an alphabet converter: You could type a name in English and get the equivalent in runes. So she typed "Trimble," and then copied the letters onto her paper:

ᛏᚱᛁᛗᛒᛚᛖ

Even though the Vikings could fool you with their *E*, which really looked a lot like an *M*, this was quite cool.

Her e-mail in-box was still empty.

Lucky copied ↑ᚠᚷᚷᚨᚱ↑: Taggart. She wrote ᚦᛗᛟᛞᛟᚱᛗ: Theodore. She wrote ↑↑↑: Triple T.

She decided to decorate the entire border of her page with her father's name written in runes. Lucky worked on this carefully and methodically, the way a scientist would do it. After a while, she realized that just drawing the very same runes that the Vikings had drawn before the eighth century gave her a distinct link to those people. Could an ancient Viking have ever imagined a girl in the twenty-first century, seated at a Formica table in a little trailer in the Mojave Desert, writing her father's name in Elder Futhark on a piece of paper with a ballpoint pen, while waiting for an e-mail? No, there were too many undiscovered and not-yet-invented things to ask those poor old Vikings to envision, and anyway, they had probably been too busy with their own lives to dream up such a weird future scene. Thinking about this, Lucky switched once again to e-mail.

Finally, a message in her in-box! It read:

> **What do you have to do with Taggart T. Trimble?**

Lucky sucked in her breath. It was almost ·magical—she'd connected with the ancient Vikings, kind of, by drawing runes, and now her father's sister was connecting with her! Because the very words of that message were proof that this *was* her aunt, since otherwise she wouldn't have known his full name was Taggart; she wouldn't have known his middle initial! Lucky wrote YAY in Elder Futhark—and was sure she could hear a whole bunch of ancient Vikings cheering in the background.

13. evidence of your credentials

Taggart Trimble is my relative.

[Lucky wrote to Siobhan Trimble Kelly]

**I need to know the names of his parents
and where they were born for an important
genealogical project. Can you help?**

Lucky read it over and decided it struck just the right note:
professional and mature.

Almost immediately, she had an answer.

**If you can provide evidence of your
credentials, I will discuss this. —STK**

Lucky rocked back in her seat, thinking, *Man, what does
she want, my birth certificate?!* And then she thought of a fact that
would prove her credentials.

He was married to Lucille P. She was my mother.

Then Lucky worried that she was revealing too much, in case this STK (or Stick, as Lucky thought of her) was some sleazy con artist, besides being her aunt. So she added:

BTW, provide evidence of YOUR credentials!

She clicked send and waited, regretting how that final sentence seemed rude, unprofessional, and immature. She could at least have said "please." Because she really, really wanted Stick to be the link to her grandparents and some great-grands, give her the names and dates, and maybe allow her to learn something about Triple T without having to interview him.

A few minutes passed, during which Lucky was pretty sure Stick was plotting her next move. Lucky wrote "Trimble" in runes under her porcupine-sledgehammer family tree, hoping it would impress Dr. Strictmund and Ms. Baum-Izzart. She glanced at Brigitte, who was concentrating on her stack of bills, punching the keys of the adding machine as if she wanted to teach them a lesson. Then, a message in her in-box:

You sound just like him. How old are you?

Feeling insulted (she did not want to sound, in any way whatsoever, like her father) but at the same time hopeful, Lucky immediately typed:

Eleven.

In seconds, a reply:

> Regarding my credentials, I assume, since
> you found me, that you already know Tag is
> my half brother. Why is an eleven-year-old
> doing genealogical research? BTW, why don't
> you ask Tag what you need to know?

Lucky pounded the Formica table with her clenched fist, causing Brigitte to glance at her and ask, "Problems, Lucky?"

"No, it's fine." *Stick, just give me a break*, she thought. Then, like peeling off a sticky bandage fast to get it over with, she typed:

> This is my penalty for fighting

Lucky deleted that and wrote instead:

> This is a school assignment. Taggart Theodore
> Trimble pays for my upkeep like when you board
> a dog at a kennel with automatic deposits so that
> way he doesn't have to think about me because
> the bank does it for him. Would YOU want to talk
> to a person like that? I don't think so. Thus

[Lucky liked the way "thus" sounded very mature]

I am asking for your help. He gave your phone number to his ex-wife, who gave it to me in case of emergency, like if he dies. He has not died that I know of but it is kind of an emergency if you see what I mean because of school.

She added:

P.S. My name is Lucky.

She hit send and immediately began to worry that Stick might misinterpret the way she compared herself to a dog being boarded in a kennel. Oh, how she hoped that this new aunt would listen with her heart!

14. a lonely little boy

"You have to give her some time, Lucky," Brigitte said. "She is not all day sitting in front of her computer. Show me this design you make on your homework."

They had finished dinner, Lucky gnawing clean the bone of her chicken leg and sopping up the deep purple sauce with a piece of bread. She saved a piece of chicken skin on the side of her plate for HMS Beagle. The Beag was allowed have a little leftover human food, but not handed to her while they were still at the table. Brigitte was very strict about that; it was a law of the house. Lucky got up to clear the plates, her dog standing at the exact same time. The Beag knew she would get a piece of chicken skin. She always had and she always would; it was another law of the house.

"It's not really a design; it's Elder Futhark." She reached across Brigitte for her homework at the end of the table. "But it's been *hours* since I wrote to 'Aunt STK.' That's like *years* in e-mail."

"Hmmm. Well, if she has still not answered in one or two days, we will call her. This is beautiful, *ma puce*, the markings. They make me think of secret buried treasure."

Lucky laughed. "I'm not your flea," she said as she always did, automatically, even though she loved being called *ma puce*. HMS Beagle went to the screen door, so Lucky opened it and then followed her outside. The Beag investigated the new kitchen foundation next to Brigitte's Westcraft trailer, a steel frame made from old rails that were once tracks for a train, cut to fit the cabin exactly. It was about the size of two king-size beds, a gigantic space compared with the trailer kitchen they were used to.

Lucky stood on the porch steps and gazed toward the Coso Range, behind which the sun would soon set. "A few days are too long to wait for an e-mail," she said to Brigitte through the screen. "People shouldn't take ages to answer; it's not polite."

Brigitte's yawn turned into a laugh. She slipped outside and hugged Lucky from behind. "The mountains are changing all the time, every minute," she said. "Have you noticed that? But always they are the same."

Lucky leaned back into the parsley smell of Brigitte. "I wonder if the ancient Vikings knew how to cook chicken like that," she said. "The Beag and I really hope so."

"*Ah, non!* They have not at all the correct recipe and they have not the ingredients, *non*." Brigitte clicked her tongue at the preposterousness of ancient Vikings making *coq au vin rouge*. Lucky smiled at the mountains. Too bad, Vikings.

When she made a final check of e-mail before bed, there was a message:

Tag is my half brother.

[Stick wrote]

My father, Sean Trimble, was married to my mother for ten years. After my parents divorced, Sean married again—an Irishwoman. They had one child, your father Taggart.

A long time ago I did a family chart. I'll try to find it and will scan and attach it in another e-mail. But it doesn't have much information on Tag's mother, Fiona (my stepmother and your grandmother), or her family, other than her own birth and death dates. I believe she was from Dublin.

Lucky felt a little thrill of triumph like when you finally press into place a piece in a gigantic difficult puzzle in which a large portion is the same color. The family tree was connecting her to people whose eyes and skin and hair and stomachs and toes and hearts were now, in some way, contained in her.

She continued reading:

You probably want to know more about your father.

Yes! Lucky thought.

Unfortunately, I cannot tell you much. When Tag was twenty-one and I was thirty-two, our father Sean died. Tag and I became involved in a lengthy legal contest over the estate, which is still not resolved. We speak to each other through our lawyers.

But I can tell you that I remember when he was born. I was exactly your age, eleven. His mother was unstable. I believe the term used now is bipolar. She had great difficulty and was institutionalized. Tag was sent to boarding schools in Europe from the age of seven. I think he was a lonely little boy. He received an excellent education and learned to speak several languages fluently, but I don't know that he was ever truly happy while he was growing up.

I did not know your mother, Lucille, but I am writing to you now because of her. When she married Tag, even though he and I were estranged, she sent me a sweet note and a beautiful miniature watercolor painting, a desert scene. I am looking at it now—it has given me a sense of peace many times over the years. I know from it that your mother was both a gifted artist and very kind.

[The message was signed]

—Siobhan Trimble Kelly

[and there was a P.S. It read]

My friends call me Stick.

15. murdock and tyson
and all the others

Like a perfect, beautiful pebble in the palm of a giant's hand, Hard Pan lay cupped in a high desert valley surrounded by hills and mountains. The sky, and there was a whole lot of it, gave the day a brilliant, beaming aspect—as if, Lucky thought, it was in a really good mood. It was exactly the right kind of day for towing a cabin from the plateau on the gouged-out, fenced-off, boarded-up hillside down into town and onto the foundation waiting for it at Brigitte's Hard Pan Café.

Lucky sprang out of bed that morning and pulled on the dark green T-shirt and leggings, lighter green shorts, and black velvet-strap flip-flops that had arrived in yesterday's mail from Mrs. Wellborne, Paloma's mom; Paloma had a matching outfit that she would also be wearing. Lucky did not have a full-length mirror but she knew she looked sort of cool, and there was a glorious sensation and smell of newness and perfectly-fittingness of everything. The bottoms of her feet loved the feel of the flip-flops' special Hawaiian sweat-absorbing straw soles. She hopped around outside for a while to let the shoes get used to her feet. It was a day that Lucky could hardly wait to plunge into, while at the same time she couldn't bear the thought of it eventually being over. It was like the moment before you open a present, still hidden inside its box and wrappings; while you're waiting to find out what it is, the eagerness and impatience and curiosity and anticipation grip you in an even stronger, more thrilling way than you feel after you find out what's inside.

Lucky wasn't the only excited person in Hard Pan. Most everyone turned out early for the occasion, a few to help with the labor, some to give warnings and advice, others to complain or to watch. Klincke Ken was chief director of operations. Dot had received permission to bring the crew onto the mine company's property so they could, as she frequently repeated, get that worthless abandoned cabin down to a place where someone could finally put it to good use. Short Sammy put his Adopt-a-Highway volunteer litter-removal equipment to work. He organized official road cones and signs to stop traffic for the brief part of the operation when the cabin would be on a public road, in case there *was* any traffic, which was highly unlikely. All the residents were staying put for the duration of the event, and no tourists would be coming to Brigitte's Hard Pan Café, which was temporarily closed.

Pete the geologist and three of his geologist friends had driven up from L.A. in work boots and hard hats; they arrived just as Justine showed up to help Brigitte with refreshments. With all the adults milling around outside, Lucky and HMS Beagle burst out of their canned-ham trailer, flung themselves down the steps, and jogged up the road. They met Lincoln at a midway point, between where the kitchen cabin was now, on the plateau by the old mine, and where it would end up, at the Café. This was the official observation station, a specially designated secure viewing area with chairs and a folding table, set up by Short Sammy on the side of the road behind a barrier of orange traffic cones.

While Lincoln and HMS Beagle, impatient for everything to get going, wandered off to investigate a flock of chukar birds, Lucky did a set of jumping jacks. She herself was perfectly calm, but her stomach was floppy; she was doing the jumping jacks to settle it. Finally Paloma and her parents, Mr. and Mrs. Wellborne, drove up. Smelling deliciously like flowers too delicate to thrive in the desert, Paloma's mom took twenty-seven pictures of the two girls in their new twin outfits; then she delivered a great deal of advice, warnings, and rules. With matching solemn expressions on their faces, Paloma and Lucky agreed to everything and said they would be very careful and always use good judgment. But Lucky was really thinking that if she ever owned elegant weightless silk clothes like Mrs. Wellborne's, she would really know how it felt to be a butterfly. And then, finally, Paloma's parents drove up to the plateau to join the other adults.

Paloma had brought something for Lucky. It was a full-page ad from the *Los Angeles Times* showing row after row and column after column of sofas, each tiny photograph identified by a name underneath. Lucky figured it fell into the same funny-without-intending-to-be-funny category as the ad tacked to her door. That ad pictured a shirtless boy making swimming motions over a bucket of water with the caption, "Learn to Swim at Home. Only $39.95 for 6 Lessons," and it had nearly made Paloma and Lucky die of severe and uncontrollable laughter on the day that they first met.

Lucky examined the dozens and dozens of sofas and shrugged, not quite getting it.

"Dorothy," Paloma said.

Lucky frowned, shaking her head.

"It's just that Dorothy looks more like a Sally to me," Paloma explained, "which, just check out the legs. Little knobs, really. Not Dorothy legs at all."

All at once, Lucky registered that the sofas had human names. Murdock and Tyson and Roger and Glenda and Bettina. She snort-laughed and then said in a serious voice, "What bothers me is that they've put Henry right between Kiki and Liz—the boy sofas and the girl sofas are all mixed together. You'd think these marketing experts would arrange them in separate sections to make it easier for customers to find what they want. For instance, some people only want the better, higher-end female sofas."

"You have a profound grasp of sofa promotion," Paloma

said in an admiring, professional tone. "May I ask if you yourself have worked in the area of sofa retailing?"

Lucky nodded. "Indeed," she said, and gazed down to the side modestly. "I've been honored by the Sofa Association of America. Lifetime Achievement Award."

Lincoln and HMS Beagle jogged back to the designated viewing area at that moment, both of them panting, as Paloma opened her eyes wide. "Wait, wait," she said. "I don't believe this. It can't be happening. Are you the world-famous sofa-namer, Lucky Trimble?"

"She's pretty famous, that's for sure," Lincoln said, as HMS Beagle gazed with adoration at Paloma, wagging her tail enthusiastically. "With at least two principals. Hey, Paloma."

"Hey, Lincoln, hey, Beag. Whoa, good dog. Yes, I am very glad to see you, too," Paloma said, giving the dog a thorough rub on her rump. She turned a little to the side, facing a pretend camera, holding a pretend microphone to her mouth. "Here we are with a renowned expert who very rarely participates in media events. Quite a treat—but first, let's ask this potential customer's opinion." Extending the pretend microphone to Lincoln, she said, "Now, would you mind telling our studio audience and the folks at home, in your own words: If you were shopping for a sofa, what would you want, a male or a female?"

Lincoln considered, then asked, "You mean for a salesperson?"

Both girls shrieked with laughter. Lincoln sighed, since he

knew from experience that he wouldn't be able to catch up with this conversation, and even if he did, he wouldn't appreciate its humor in the same extreme way they did.

So then Lucky told Paloma more about the session in the principal's office, which they had already e-mailed briefly about, while Lincoln and HMS Beagle stood by, the four of them hanging out (under strict instructions from Klincke Ken not to go anywhere else along the road where the cabin procession would take place). They were waiting for the crew up on the plateau to finish getting the cabin ready to be moved: They had to jack it up off the ground, using a whole bunch of car jacks, then jam telephone poles underneath to support the floor, then drive the dolly into loading position. They had to chain the cabin securely in place on the dolly, haul it down the dirt road, turn at the spot where the four waited, and finally unload it at the Café.

Paloma had also heard about the family tree punishment and the amazing discovery of Lucky's father's half sister. She asked, "So did that aunt tell you anything good?"

"First she sent me an e-mail with something like, 'What is your interest in Tag Trimble?' I was calling her Stick because her initials are STK, and that's how she was acting, just like an old stick. But then it turned out that her friends really do call her Stick, and she's kind of nice, I mean, the last thing I expected was that she'd be really *quite* nice, but she is."

"I *so* wish I had an aunt," Paloma said. Both her parents were only children, as was Paloma herself. "I think of an aunt as almost like an older sister, except they're always nice and you don't have to fight over who gets the remote."

"I've got eight aunts, counting my parents' three sisters plus the wives of their five brothers," Lincoln said. "They're all great, but the downside is it means a zillion thank-you notes every birthday." This was a definite disadvantage Lucky hadn't considered before; a letter-writing burden like that would be torture. She decided her current three were a perfect amount of aunts to have. Suddenly she wondered if Ollie Martin was also discovering brand-new relatives.

As often happened, Lincoln read her mind. He said, "Mom said last night that Ollie already finished his maternal side. He's got everyone back to the great-greats."

Ollie's progress on his family tree infuriated Lucky.

"I wish Stick lived closer. I'd go pound on her door and make her tell me *ev-ree-thing* she knows."

Lincoln smiled and said, "Hey, if she doesn't tell you *ev-ree-thing*, you could throw her your special jaw-breaker punch." Lucky knew he was teasing her, since the whole point, the reason she was having to dredge up relatives, was that she'd socked Ollie Martin in the first place.

"What about Lucille and her parents?" Paloma asked.

"My maternal grands died when I was a baby. Lincoln's mom showed me where to write to get copies of the death certificates, which will have the names of all *their* parents and where they were born. So then I'll be done with *that* whole side of the tree." Lucky said this the way you would talk about being done with the type of impossible math problem where if A dies when $X = 8$ and $X = (A + C) + B$, then what is the higher power of X? It made her brain feel a little tired and sad, so she was glad to move on from the maternals.

16. a french *ado*

The sudden appearance of a car at the crest of the paved high-way where the road descended into Hard Pan made everyone look west, where their shadows pointed. Lucky and Lincoln recognized it immediately: Stu Burping in his official Inyo County Health Department vehicle. As he drove straight to where the little group was waiting, they saw that Ollie Martin was once again in the passenger seat.

"Oh, boy," Lucky said, with a lot of irony in her voice. She and Paloma both had begun using a great deal of irony, which they explained to their mothers was an extremely sophisticated form of humor.

Paloma looked at her with an ironic expression. "Don't tell me that's the guy you got into a fight with, which, what's *he* doing here?"

"He's the county health inspector's nephew," Lincoln said.

Stu Burping drove up and got out of the car, smelling of

V8 juice, adjusting his cap. "This is a great day for Hard Pan!" he proclaimed, adding, "I'll be honest with you—I made Ollie come with me." Ollie sat with his arm hanging out the window, staring straight ahead in a grim and resentful way. "Thought maybe you kids should get to know each other. Can you all handle it?"

This was another example, in Lucky's opinion, of where adult thinking can be just plain screwy. "Right," she said.

"Right," Lincoln said.

"Right," Paloma said.

Ollie lumbered out of the car, slamming the door. "Right," he sighed, and lowered one end of his skateboard to the black-top, where his right foot took control, levering it in various directions. He was wearing a tight black T-shirt, cutoff jeans, knee pads, and elbow pads.

Despite her pain-in-the-neck family-tree punishment for having hit him, Lucky had an impulse to whap Ollie again. He had that same obnoxious way of showing off with his skateboard and all his gear, as if he were bored just by the fact of sharing the same planet as you.

It made her want to force him to lick ants off a rotten apple and swallow them.

"Hey, Ollie," Lincoln said in a neutral, not unfriendly voice.

"Hey, Lincoln." Ollie offered a little tilted-chin junior high type of guy-greeting. Lucky rolled her eyes at Paloma, who stood off to one side. Paloma winked back at her.

Lincoln said, "You might as well know we've been given

our orders: All of us kids have to stay behind these refreshment tables. We're under Klincke Ken's command. He'll stop the operation if he sees any of us budging from this spot."

"Good plan," Stu Burping said. His tired-looking old brown shoes made Lucky feel a little pity for his feet because they were probably tired too. "Ollie, you got that, right? Stay here until Klincke Ken gives the signal that it's okay to disperse. I'm going up where the crew is with the cabin, see if they need any help. You"—he swept his official county supervisor eyes over each of them—"stay out of trouble."

After he left, Brigitte and Justine drove up with a pizza; more refreshments were waiting at the end, but Brigitte said she thought some of the observers might like a little snack. You could smell it through the Jeep's open windows, and even if you hadn't been hungry before, you wanted a piece. But Lucky noticed that Ollie wasn't looking at the food as Justine set it out on the folding table; he didn't see her spinning the wheel of a pizza knife or tapping a rapid beat with it on the edge of the table. No, Ollie was gawking at Brigitte. He stared as she and Paloma hugged and gave each other kisses on both cheeks.

Then Brigitte smiled at him. Lucky couldn't believe her eyes. She smiled at the enemy! Even knowing, because Lucky had told her, everything: how that jerk had insulted the Café, the lies he had told. And then to Lucky's further disgust, Brigitte said, "Olivier?" like she was glad to see him. He nodded and blushed. Well, this wasn't new—everyone who met Brigitte was dazzled by her beauty, how she always looked fresh and energetic, no matter how hot it was or how hard she worked. Lucky had gotten used to that. But how could her mother be nice to him?

"It is what I suspected," Brigitte said, gazing into Ollie's eyes while Lucky and Paloma gaped at her. "His mouth. Definitely."

Paloma eyebrowed Lucky as a way of saying, *What is she talking about?* And Lucky eyebrowed back, saying, *I haven't got a clue!*

Apparently Ollie didn't get it either, and probably thought she was making fun of him, because he folded his arms and looked off toward the cabin on the plateau, where all the other grown-ups were clustered. Justine, frowning and squinting, also gazed in that direction.

"Olivier Martin," Brigitte said. But it sounded as if she were speaking French, not English. She pronounced his last name *Mar-TAN*.

"No," he said. "MAR-tin. *Oliver* MAR-tin."

Brigitte shrugged and offered him a slice of pizza. Glancing sideways at Lucky, who narrowed her eyes to remind him of *rat-burgers*, he said, "Um, it's cool. I'm not hungry." But Lucky saw him wanting pizza, and she was glad.

"We know from your mouth," Brigitte said, "because you have no lips, and from that large nose, that your ancestor was from France. You look just like a French *ado*."

He sighed in an annoyed way, and Lucky knew it was because he couldn't figure Brigitte out. She was acting really nice and interested in him, but she said stuff he didn't get. And what about having no lips and a big nose? That seemed insulting, but she didn't say it in an insulting way; she said it more like a compliment.

He was trapped, Lucky realized happily, because he wasn't allowed up on the plateau, and he was forced by Stu Burping to hang out. There were no low walls he could try to bully people off of, no smooth sidewalk for tricks. He rocked on his skateboard, scowling.

"What's an *ado*, Brigitte?" Paloma asked.

"An adolescent." She pronounced it the French way, *ad-o-less-ONT*.

"Adolescent?" Ollie asked.

Brigitte raised her eyebrows. "It is what I just said."

"Why don't you say it in American, then?" Ollie asked.

Lucky snorted. "In *English*," she corrected. "American isn't a language."

Brigitte said, "But you understand me, the way I pronounce this word, Olivier, yes?" Ollie nodded. Lucky noticed that his ears had turned red.

"Brigitte," Paloma wondered, "why do you call him Olivier instead of Oliver?"

"I tell you already. Because he is French. In France, Martin is a common family name, like Smith is here. We know a family of Martins when I am a girl."

"I'm American. I'm the most American person here."

Then Paloma did a weird thing. She strode over to stand

directly in front of Ollie. She peered closely at his face. "Brigitte's right, Lucky," she said, as if he were a painting and she was an art historian. "He has no lips and quite a large nose." She looked into his eyes. "Oh," she said, "by the way, I'm Paloma Alta Wellborne."

Ollie took a step back. "Like the Alta Wellborne Studios in Hollywood?"

Paloma glanced up toward where her father was showing off his new Cadillac Escalade hybrid SUV to some of the onlookers, and where her mother, silk scarf and dress fluttering in the breeze, was talking with Dot. She sighed. "Hollywood, New York, London, Toronto, and Sydney, yes. But that is not the point." She stepped again very close to Ollie, her beautiful droopy eyes narrowed. "The point is, my ancestors are from England and Mexico, which, my mom's a Mexican citizen and an American. The point is, I love Hard Pan. I love Brigitte and her Hard Pan Café. The *point*, Ollie, is that Miles and Lincoln are my friends and Lucky's *dog* is my friend and Lucky herself"—she paused, took a breath—"is my best friend on earth." She waited, looking him straight in the eyes. "Did you get all that?"

He nodded and stopped rocking on his skateboard. He was big and gangly, like his bones had grown too fast. He looked a little bit intimidated, as if Paloma scared him.

"Then have some pizza and shut up," Paloma said, and Brigitte handed him a slice, laughing.

"Well," Lincoln said, straight-faced, to Ollie, "looks like it was a good thing you wore all that safety gear."

"Safety gear," Justine repeated, frowning, as she spun the wheel of the pizza cutter. Lucky was used to the way that Justine was always tapping or clicking or rapping or flicking—making little noises not on purpose but because the engine inside her seemed to operate at a faster speed, like the whirring of a hummingbird's wings.

Brigitte turned to her. "What? Justine, something is wrong?"

Justine rubbed her arms like someone trying to warm herself, though the temperature was already up close to the eighties. "It's Miles. He's supposed to be here. He said he'd meet me right here. I shouldn't be worried, since the kingdom of heaven is within him, within all of us, right this minute. But this morning he got so mad at me. We argued when I explained that he cannot have a burro of his own." Justine touched the gelled tips of her spiky hair. "He's been asking for days and days, and he won't listen when I say no. So he stomped outside just before I came by to help with the refreshments. I haven't seen him for over an hour."

Brigitte touched Justine's arm and said, "Probably you do not need to worry. All the people in Hard Pan love Miles and watch out for him. It is like Lucky is saying always to me: What is the worst thing that can happen?"

Shouts from the crew up on the plateau by the mine made all seven of them (including HMS Beagle) turn to look, as a Caterpillar engine rumbled and began very slowly to tow a slat-sided wooden cabin down the dirt road to where they were waiting.

Paloma gripped Lucky's hands. "Here it comes!" she said.
"Let's be the Hard Pan cabin-moving cheerleader team!"

Although they had occasional slight difficulties with their new flip-flops because they tended to fly off during sideways leg kicks (which was very exciting to HMS Beagle), all in all their jumping jacks and other moves were nicely coordinated and very enthusiastic. Lucky knew both Lincoln and Ollie were watching them as much as the cabin-moving, and she felt pretty sure that she and Paloma looked every bit as cool as real junior high cheerleaders, if not cooler.

17. a glitch

Everything was going fine with the operation. The Cat loader slowly gained speed and momentum as it towed its cargo down the hill. The star of the event, the cabin itself, looked prettily old-fashioned, with its wood-shingle roof and clapboard siding. Every member of the crew was shouting directions, questions, comments, and orders to every other member of the crew. They were having a wonderful time.

Klincke Ken wasn't worried about the brake problem, the problem being that the loader didn't have any. He wasn't worried because he'd planned it all out. The kids were out of the way, safely behind the designated viewing area. The other spectators had been ordered to stay *well behind* the trailer and under *no circumstances whatsoever* to go in front of his loader. He would simply sail along at a reasonable pace; there was no need to come to a standstill anywhere on his route. And once he arrived at the destination, he'd ease the Caterpillar in low gear up an ingenious inclined ramp that he'd built especially for this purpose. The ramp would bring the loader to a stop. Since he knew it would all go as planned, Klincke Ken had not seen any point in telling anyone that the salvaged towing vehicle had no brakes.

He sat in the driver's seat and flashed a huge, brand-new, triumphant Grizzle White Enamel smile as he sailed down the road. The cabin, nearly as wide as the dirt road, lumbered along behind him on its dolly made from parts off the abandoned eighteen-wheeler and the lowboy trailer, the clapboard walls creaking, shingled roof flapping, windows rattling, chains whipping, huge tires grinding into the pavement. The noise was deafening. It was a glorious spectacle. A line of dusty vehicles and crew and onlookers followed in Klincke Ken's wake, looking like a Fourth of July parade that had been lost for a long, long time in the desert.

Lucky saw movement to her right, out of the corner of her eye, and she turned toward it just as Lincoln did. A small orange animal in the distance was darting across the road.

"Kirby!" Lincoln said. It was Klincke Ken's little ginger mouser.

Following a few yards behind the cat was Chesterfield, who had clearly escaped his bedspring fence. Chesterfield was similar to all burros in that he did not care to be told what to do. He liked to do what *he* wanted to do. And apparently he did *not* want to be in Klincke Ken's yard, but *did* want to be in the middle of the road. Because when he came to an exactly perfect middle-of-the-road spot, he stopped. And that is where he stayed. He crooked one leg at the ankle, like a gentleman waiting for his turn at golf, and swished a fly with his tail. Kirby curled up in the shady place on the ground under his belly. She understood that Chesterfield had found the one good spot—not a little ahead nor a little back but right there. Naturally, all *she* wanted was to share that spot with him.

Since Lucky was squinting straight toward the bright mid-morning sun, she couldn't be sure, but it seemed as if Chesterfield had an extra pair of legs—or was it some kind of shadow movement—something on the burro's other side. She used her two hands to shade her eyes, frowning, finally realizing that the head belonging to the extra legs was obscured by Chesterfield's great head, and that the extra legs could belong to only one short unaccounted-for person: Miles.

The official viewing station was situated where the dirt road from the plateau at the mine met the paved road into Hard Pan, allowing people there a clear view both of the cabin's starting place and all along the trajectory, like the leg of an L that continued downhill toward Brigitte's Hard Pan Café. They could see the crew as it accompanied the cabin down from the plateau, and they could see Chesterfield fifty or sixty yards to the east. But because there were shacks and trailers and houses along the present part of his route, Klincke Ken could not yet see his beloved cat and burro right in the middle of the road he was

about to turn onto, nor the small boy on the other side of the burro. But what he could see was that the loaded-up cab was moving faster than he expected.

Ollie saw it too. "It's fast," he said. "That burro better move it."

He tossed his skateboard on the road and tore off toward Chesterfield, one foot churning the blacktop as his skateboard gained momentum. With the Beag at her side, Lucky broke into a run after Ollie, calling back something over her shoulder, ignoring Brigitte's "Stop!"

Justine grabbed Brigitte's hand. "What did she say? Something about Miles? Do you see him? I don't have my glasses." She squinted in Lucky's direction.

Paloma yelled out, "Oh, my God, he's in the road—he's on

the other side of that burro—" She began waving her arms and shouting, "Get back! Get back!"

Justine cried out as Brigitte called, "Lucky!" and then both of them were also flying down the road, Justine in the lead.

Lincoln darted across the pavement, just in front of where the approaching Cat and its load would make the wide turn.

"Lincoln!" Paloma screamed across at him. "What are you doing? Why isn't Klincke Ken slowing down?"

"I'm jumping aboard while he makes the turn," Lincoln shouted back. "May need help!" He meant, of course, Klincke Ken.

But Paloma thought he meant that *he* might need help, so she nodded, readying herself to climb on from her side as the contraption rounded the turn.

18. an unexpected outcome

Klincke Ken took the corner just a bit too abruptly, which caused the whole building to shift. The cabin was chained to the phone poles and to the dolly, but the chains were not ratcheted too tightly, allowing for a little movement. Not enough for the cabin to slip off, but enough for it to tip and to slide out a bit over the edge of its platform.

Since he was so busy overcorrecting the imbalance this caused, and a great deal of advice and warnings were being hollered by the bystanders who trotted along behind—not that Klincke Ken paid the slightest attention to them—he didn't notice Lincoln and Paloma on either side of him. But as Lincoln had guessed, turning the corner forced Klincke Ken to downshift and the loader to slow down to the pace of a slow jog, making it possible to hop on. The gigantic rear tires of the loader presented a logistical problem: You had to avoid those tires. However, there was a space behind them, behind Klincke Ken in the driver's seat, where, by trotting alongside and gripping the edge and then jamming one foot onto a little low metal platform, a person with good timing could scramble aboard. Paloma obviously had the same idea. She tore her leggings, lost a flip-flop, stubbed her toe, and scraped her knee, and Lincoln, trying to favor his injured right wrist, banged his elbow—but both of them managed to climb up and hang on.

The cabin-moving crew and spectators were triumphant at the success and brilliance of the first and most problematic leg of the project. As they reached the now deserted official observation area, they figured the kids had gone on to wait at the cabin's final destination; their view ahead was blocked by the cabin itself. So they continued following along behind in a straggly bunch, discussing the finer points of Klincke Ken's achievements so far.

All except Mrs. Wellborne, who was alarmed on not finding Paloma at the viewing station, where she was supposed to be. She had a terrible blinding worry about Paloma, so she took off her elegant shoes and trotted barefoot in the sand bordering the road, dodging bushes and snake holes, trying to maneuver around Klincke Ken and his load in order to get ahead of it.

In her mind, timed to the slapping of her flip-flops on the pavement, Lucky heard a chant. The words burned in the flame of her original what-if-the-Café-disappeared thought that had then led to the visit of the county health department inspector.

As she pounded toward Miles and the animals, the words drummed in her ears. *What-if, what-if, what-if, what-if.* What if Klincke Ken's contraption couldn't stop in time? What if people got killed? It would all be her fault. *Her fault, her fault, her fault, her fault.* She ran faster.

And then, to her amazement, Justine shot by, zooming ahead easily.

And ahead of *her*, Miles was trying to get Chesterfield to move off the road. He must have seen how close Klincke Ken was, and he was not going to leave Chesterfield in its path, no matter what. He was being so typically Miles! And why the heck wasn't Klincke Ken slowing down? Was he crazy? Didn't he see them? And at that moment, her flip-flop came down on a rock. Her ankle buckled and she flew forward, flat on her face.

Klincke Ken gave the loader some gas as he came out of the turn. He was feeling thrilled, exultant, and optimistic. After wrestling with the Cat's gears and its steering wheel, he felt he had the unwieldy cabin steady again, and not in danger of slipping off. But suddenly there were two kids right behind him, climbing onto his loader—what in tarnation? Then he saw it was only Lincoln and a girl, but still he was thrown by this unplanned-for event. He twisted around to frown at Lincoln, who shouted, "Help?" which just plain made Klincke Ken mad. People asked him for help all the time, and usually he was happy to do what he could, but *right now*? *At a time like this*? He was let down,

shaken, disappointed to realize that Lincoln—always a serious, smart boy—was not being more respectful of the importance of this operation.

"Later!" Klincke Ken shouted. "I'm a little busy!" He resolved to ignore those two and turned back around to face front and the home stretch. And what he saw caused him to rise up in his seat. Kids! And women! Half the blasted town, it looked like—all over the road! One boy ahead of the others on a skateboard; then Justine, it looked like, with HMS Beagle streaking beside her; then someone—it must be Lucky—who was down, lying on the road near the side; and Brigitte pulling up the rear, and zigzagging behind them but thank God off-road, another woman in a billowing dress. And what they were all running toward about fifty yards ahead was that little boy Miles, and *he* was pulling on . . . Chesterfield! Klincke Ken felt his heart thump hard against his chest, like it was trying to get out. Chesterfield! And Kirby! Right in the middle of the street.

He glanced to his left. Trailers and houses lined the road, big liquid propane tanks between each building. The other side was the desert, after a soft shoulder and a sandy drop of about four feet. Klincke Ken faced the horror of his situation. He could not stop the loader. If he drove to the left, anybody inside those houses would be killed and he'd certainly rip into one of the propane tanks, causing an explosion and massive fire. If he plowed straight ahead, he'd hit Chesterfield, Kirby, and women and children. If he drove off the road to the right, where he'd seen many upside-down vehicles over the years, the weight and momentum of the cabin and dolly would cause them, and naturally the Cat, to flip over. The two kids behind him would fly off and get their necks broke, or they'd get crushed, all three of them would, under the vehicle. So Klincke Ken gripped the wheel and pressed on, panic-stricken, stunned, and desperate for a miracle.

Ollie sped on, knees bent, taking advantage of the downhill slope of the blacktop, maneuvering as best he could along its rough surface. His plan was to leap his board—to do an ollie—just as he passed behind the burro, and as he sailed by he'd slap the animal's rump hard to make it get the heck off the road.

But before he even had a chance to do this, the sound that his skateboard wheels made—a loud grating noise Chesterfield

had never heard and did not care for in the least—gave the
burro a bad opinion of the developing situation. Another thing
Chesterfield did not like was the way the boy was coming up
very fast behind him. The reaction was instinctive, a reflex that
burros have perfected over the thousands of years they've lived
among humans. And Chesterfield timed his move exactly, kicking out with his back legs at exactly the right moment. He just
wanted that fast-moving noisy boy to quit bothering him. Fortunately for Ollie, those powerful hooves made contact with the
skateboard rather than directly with the boy, who flew backward
and landed on a pile of abandoned rimless tires on the side of
the road.

Kirby objected. Too much kicking, shouting, running,
noise, commotion! She wailed and skittered away toward home.
This electrified Chesterfield, who bolted after her.

Then Justine reached the scene. She scooped up Miles under one arm and dove to the desert side of the road, followed by HMS Beagle, the three of them rolling to a breathless, gasping stop on soft sand.

Lucky, having just fallen, lay in a kind of trance, the breath knocked out of her and no new breath coming for what seemed a long while; one part of her knew she needed to get up but another part decided it would wait for another few minutes until her thoughts got clearer. Then a cry broke through, and at the same time Lucky felt herself being yanked off the road, grasped under her arms by Brigitte's strong hands. A second later, as she and Brigitte looked up, the loader and its cargo charged by. Mrs. Wellborne, stopping for breath, turned in sur-prise to see her daughter standing behind the driver, sailing past.

In the time it took Klincke Ken to blink, the road before him had become wondrously clear. He believed it was a miracle. One second the great mass of machinery bore down on people and animals and the next second not a boy, not a girl, not a woman, not a dog, cat, nor burro in sight. Klincke Ken pressed on ahead, certain he didn't deserve the good fortune that had just come his way but glad to accept it. The two in the loader behind him cheered loudly. Klincke Ken didn't even hear them as he contemplated the glory and the terror all of them had just survived. The sky had never in his life been so blue, the air so pure, or the sun so brilliant.

Finally the Caterpillar wheezed to a stop a few yards short of its destination, having run out of gas due to a second slight miscalculation of Klincke Ken's. Several pickup trucks took over, chaining the cabin to their rear tow bars. In a kind of dusty, noisy truck ballet, the vehicles coordinated their moves, inching the cabin off the dolly with a shrieking of joists and clanking of chains and revving of engines, up the slight ramp and onto the steel rail foundation. The little cabin extended the C shape of the three soldered-together trailers. They formed a curve like a crescent moon, with the Café tables grouped in its hollow and the great Mojave Desert beyond, all the way to the horizon.

While these final maneuvers were going on, everyone who had been involved in rescuing Miles, Chesterfield, and Kirby, plus rescuers who had themselves become rescuees, got wiped off, cleaned up, bandaged, congratulated, admonished, reproached, and admired. Lucky and Paloma escaped into the crowd as soon as they could. Mrs. Wellborne soaked her feet in a basin of warm water with Epsom salts as Mr. Kennedy tried to reassure her that, whereas Lincoln's and Paloma's acrobatics had been a bit risky, the two of them had shown courage and ingenuity and heroism. Mrs. Wellborne said she preferred virtues like being sensible, cautious, and careful. Mr. Kennedy confided that, in fact, he worried about Lincoln going off to England all alone. So then it was Mrs. Wellborne's turn to cheer *him* up by reminding him that Lincoln was a fine, smart, thoughtful boy.

Mr. Wellborne and Brigitte arrived with glasses of champagne for a toast to the Café. And they all had a sip and agreed that growing up is tough, especially for the parents.

Meanwhile, Klincke Ken, Short Sammy, Pete, and Stu Burping examined the cabin all around. They tramped inside with spirit levels and plumb bobs and straightedges. They came back out and declared the building safe and sound. A cheer went up as Lucky and Paloma sprinted in, followed by Brigitte, followed by everyone else, so the girls soon popped outside again for air.

"It's *great*," Paloma said as they limped backward—they had matching stubbed big toes—for more of a distance view, "which, I can't believe how *huge* it seems."

"Pal," said Lucky, "check out the hero over there."

Ollie was reenacting the morning's adventures, with Miles playing the parts of Chesterfield, Kirby, and himself. Justine was hugging both boys, and Mrs. Prender was providing cold sun tea. Lucky said, "Do you believe this? I'm sure that both of *us* are going to get in trouble later—'you need to make better choices, you need to use better judgment'—right?" Lucky folded her arms—her skin burns resembled Ollie's skateboard road rash—like a seriously angry principal. "But do the *guys* get in trouble? Not that *I* noticed."

Paloma laughed and draped an arm over Lucky's shoulders. "You're right," she said, "which, I bet the person who thought up sofa naming was a guy. 'Hey, this dark blue tweed high-armed, round-footed sofa isn't just a sofa. It's Bertha!'"

Lucky said, "So the other sofa people go, 'Whoa, this man is a genius!'"

"What man?" Lincoln asked, coming up to them, but they were laughing so hard they couldn't answer.

An unfortunate casualty of the day was Ollie's skateboard, which had been cracked by Chesterfield's hooves and smashed by the loader's massive tires. Plus, Ollie had collected some bruises and a sprained wrist, so Lincoln lent him a spare brace. But Ollie, explaining to Brigitte that she could call him Olivier if she wanted, because in fact it was true that his paternal side was full of French people, and that his great-grandparents had immigrated to the United States, seemed to have lightened up. Somehow his brief, eventful, heroic day and the discovery that he looked like a French *ado* had completely changed his outlook.

He ate a great deal of Brigitte's pizza and mini quiches and submitted smilingly to a fair amount of her teasing. Ollie now saw quite clearly that people at Einstein Junior High just didn't realize what a cool place Hard Pan actually was.

117

19. a very old story

You could smell how strongly the new kitchen cabin was becoming fortified against enemy invaders. A fresh coat of paint on the walls, mineral oil for the wood sills and moldings, and Murphy Oil Soap mixed with hot water for the floor. If Lucky were an ant, she wouldn't dare set foot inside, but to her human nose, the mixture smelled like *welcome*.

She scraped gunk from a windowsill and dug a few facts about Triple T out of Brigitte, who had to be prodded and cajoled to talk about him. "My version of him," she explained to Lucky, "is short, exciting, and it is sad."

"I know," Lucky had answered patiently. "Just tell me about meeting him and what he was like. Did he ever say anything about his parents?"

"*Non,*" Brigitte said, jamming her sponge mop into a corner, her back to Lucky. She was scouring every inch of the wood plank floor. "Except that his *maman* was not well for most of her life."

Lucky already knew about that, thanks to Stick, and she knew her grandmother Fiona was born in Ireland. She poured a few drops of mineral oil onto her clean rag and rubbed it into the wood of the sill, careful not to allow any drips.

"So he was in Paris studying for a year at the university," Lucky said, trying to get the engine of Brigitte's memory started the same way the Captain usually got his van going by giving it a push downhill.

"Yes, at the Sorbonne. I am working at the pastry shop nearby, where he comes each day to buy a croissant. He is so American! Friendly but not in a flirting way, very polite." Brigitte plunged her mop into a bucket of hot water and Murphy Oil

Soap. "I do not know Americans before him, except for movies. To me—" She squeezed the mop, dipped it in the water, squeezed again. "To me, he is exotic because of being so . . . open. Normally in France we are more reserved. He smiles with all his teeth," she explained, "like you."

"Okay, so you went on a date?"

"*Non*, we just have coffee because I am not sure about him. His French is very good, but formal and old-fashioned. He uses some words from the nineteenth century that no one says today. They are like antique words." She frowned, thinking. "He has a quality of being a gentleman, and I like this very much. Look up there, a *faucheux*—a daddy longlegs. *Always* in the corner is another daddy longlegs." She went after it with her mop.

120   Lucky was very interested in daddy longlegs but refused to let the subject veer off into a discussion of them. "A gentleman like how?" She rubbed the wood window frame vigorously, as if only half-interested in the conversation. If she showed her eagerness, if she was not *reserved* like French people, Brigitte might cut the story short.

"Oh, I remember I tell him I have the dream to become a chef, but it is an impossible dream—very difficult to do this in France. The next day he brings me a present. It is a book, very old, of Escoffier, the first great chef of France." Brigitte resumed mopping under the table. "I think with this book he is telling me how much he respects our tradition of cooking, and also that because I am French I inherit the tradition; that I can become a chef. It makes me fall in love—with that simple view of the world, and a little bit with him."

"Hmmm," Lucky said. "So then?"

"Oh, Lucky, it is a very old story. He is handsome, very smart—like you—he tells about California, how beautiful it is, how he loves me." She plunged the mop down, hard, into the bucket again. "Here is the truth. It is my fault the marriage does not work."

"*Your* fault? How could it be your fault?"

"I tell you already. Now listen, because I do not want to talk about this again."

Lucky nodded, waiting, almost afraid to breathe. HMS Beagle, banished to the small front porch while Brigitte mopped, could be heard sighing loudly in her sleep.

Brigitte leaned the mop against a wall; her faded blue scrunchie had come loose. She removed it, tilting her head back and gathering her hair into a ponytail, looping the scrunchie around it. Lucky wished she could inherit Brigitte's beautiful high cheekbones and finely arched dark eyebrows, though of course she could not, being adopted. But maybe she'd be able, somehow, to absorb Brigitte's way of looking confident and radiant, even with a mop in her hands and a faded scrunchie in her hair.

"Before we marry I tell him I want to have a child. He does not want children, and he is very clear, very . . . emphatic. But I am young and I make the mistake of thinking I can change his mind. Secretly, I feel sure he will one day agree with what I want. I was wrong."

"So that was it?"

"Well, not entirely. It was . . . very difficult because we have fun, we like the same music, my *maman* adores him and says he is a good husband for me. But I am too sad, thinking always of my life with no child. He will not change; I will not change. So we agree to divorce."

Lucky thought, *And then he came back to California and married Lucille, who must not have cared that Triple T didn't want a child, because* she *became pregnant.*

Brigitte was obviously thinking the same thoughts. She said, "And this is the wonderful paradox. He gives me a beautiful American child, after all: you."

Lucky felt strangely like crying, partly because the story was so sad but also because it was so confusing. Triple T had not behaved as badly as she'd thought—he had been thoughtful and honest (and fun!) with Brigitte.

The window's rough old wood frame had soaked up half a bottle of mineral oil; it now looked rich and smooth. Brigitte said she was smart, like her father, and Lucky breathed in that thought—mingled with the new kitchen cabin's comforting scent.

20. when god was six

Miles kicked one of the four washing machines lined up in front of his grandmother's house. "I'm not discussing dinosaurs with you, Lucky! Or you, either, Lincoln," he said, gripping a half-eaten hot dog until his fingers left indentations in the bun and mustard and ketchup surged out onto his hand. "Except it says in the Bible that *everything* on Earth, including the dinosaurs, was created at the same time."

Lincoln and Lucky sat eating their own hot dogs on two of the washing machines not being kicked. "But, Miles," Lincoln

said, "what about those books you read about the Jurassic and those other periods. Remember how you always told us about how the dinosaurs existed for millions of years before the early hominids? And the fossil finds where they discovered new species? What happened to all that scientific evidence?"

"Shut up!" Miles shouted. "Justine even showed me a museum you can go to online that shows how all the animals and everything were being created on Earth at the same time. All the animals." Like everyone else, Miles called his mother Justine.

Lucky frowned. It was pretty unusual to see Miles so angry and upset. She said, "Well, the Bible was written by people, right? And people make mistakes, don't they? Like, in those days they hadn't found any ancient skeletons or fossils and they didn't know about evolution. They didn't even know about the dinosaurs."

"They weren't making mistakes. The Bible is the word of God." Miles picked up a fist-size rock and threw it, hard, at the base of the washing machine serving as a perch for Lucky.

"Hey, come on, quit that, Miles," she said. "Listen, calm down and think about this for a second, okay? What if God was just a kid your age at the time of the Bible being written? Like say he was about six. So even though he's God, he's still figuring out how everything's going to work. Because it's, like, our Earth is his first project and he's kind of making it up as he goes along."

Miles lobbed another stone, but this time he aimed at an

upside-down tin tub. It pinged off the side. "God was never six," he said, but he didn't sound sure.

"Well," Lincoln put in, "but say Lucky's right. He's really young in God-years at the time of Adam and Eve."

"God-years?" Lucky made an *Is this supposed to be helpful?* face at Lincoln.

"In the context of eternity, Lucky," Lincoln said, with a *Would you just listen for a second?* look back at her. "Like a zillion of our years might be the bat of an eye for God, and the six days of creation would be zillions of our human years."

"Kind of like we say dog years," Lucky said slowly, catching on. "HMS Beagle is middle-aged in dog years, even though she's only six in our years, and you're six too, Miles, but you're still a kid. Or just think of what six years would be like to a daddy longlegs—say he's doing his family tree, six years for him would be something like me having to go back a thousand generations."

Lincoln added, "And Pete and the geologists don't even think in years. They talk about eons because geologic time is in *millions* of years. Maybe God-years are like eons, so immense we can hardly imagine them. See what I mean?"

Miles didn't answer. After a moment Lincoln continued, "Yeah, anyway. So God decides to make the Bible as a kind of owner's manual or how-to guide. He tells certain people what to write and you get the books of the Old Testament and then the New Testament. Right? But maybe for some reason he decided not to tell them about the dinosaurs and other extinct animals;

they had been living eons earlier, so I don't know, maybe it wasn't something God felt like going into right then."

Lucky smiled at Lincoln. "He'd outgrown his dinosaur phase," she said.

"Or he figured the early people had enough on their minds already." Lincoln waved his hot dog in a big arc, indicating the vastness of the world. "Or maybe he *wanted* us to find out later, on our own, so he made us smart enough to invent science and to make instruments."

Miles glared at them. "It's really wrong to talk about God that way." He opened one of the washing machines and threw the remains of his hot dog inside, slamming the lid and wiping his hand on his jeans. "Quit doing that and accept Jesus," he went on, resting his cheek against the flaky greenish metal top of the machine, "so you can be here on the final day and enter heaven!"

"Miles," Lincoln said. "Listen. Just think about this. Why *wouldn't* God let Lucky and me into heaven?"

"We all sin," said Miles. "Everybody. But it's like Justine says—we can all be saved anyway, by taking Jesus into our hearts. And all the people who already died, if they took Jesus as their savior, they get to come back to life on Earth."

"Well, that's the other thing," Lucky said, licking ketchup off the palm of her hand, "how *crowded* that sounds, with heaven being on Earth, if you have all those people who died coming back. I mean, *if* they took Jesus as their savior. Did you ask Justine how there'll be enough room for everyone?"

Miles nodded, sideways, his head pressed against the machine. "Yes, but I don't like explaining this," he moaned.

"Come on, Miles—I don't get it. There may be tens of gazillions of people. How is everybody going to fit?"

"No oceans," Miles mumbled.

"No oceans?"

"They cover seventy percent of the Earth's surface. Without them there'll be room for everyone." Miles recited this in a practiced way, Lucky thought, as if he had it memorized. But it sounded more like he was trying to believe it than like he actually did, and he reminded her of someone about to get a shot with a giant needle, looking the other way until it's over.

21. how lucky would cope if she had to

Lucky worried a little bit, from time to time, that Brigitte would die. It was hard to think of the world without Brigitte in it, because Brigitte filled up a day the way air fills up a room. If she died, Lucky's life would just suck into itself and collapse, like when you force air out of a Ziploc bag. So mostly when these worries came into Lucky's head, what she had to do was envision Brigitte's old mother. It seemed that as long as the old mother was alive, Brigitte couldn't die—it would not make sense, because old people are supposed to die first.

On Sunday evening, after a long, hard, busy weekend of making jams and sauces that could be preserved, Brigitte pulled off her apron as if it were as heavy as the kind you have to wear when you get an X-ray at the dentist. She dropped it on the floor and kicked off her espadrilles, limping into her bedroom trailer. "Ten minutes," she said, and fell backward onto her bed. Lucky stood there, amazed: They hadn't even finished wiping down the counters. Brigitte fell asleep instantly, lying on her back like a

128

doll, its lifeless head on the pillow. Lucky watched, alarmed and wondering if she should call Short Sammy, who was connecting the water lines in the new kitchen cabin next door. It was like seeing a limp goldfish: strange and scary. Lucky had never realized how Brigitte was all about fluid motion, so different from the nervous repetitive tapping of Justine. Brigitte's face, limbs, and body moved as she talked and as she worked and even as she listened, but in sleep all that action drained into a deep stillness. Lucky leaned in close to reassure herself that Brigitte was still breathing and hadn't died. And then, under almost translucent eyelids, the two round eyeballs twitched. Lucky tiptoed outside with her soapy sponge. She scrubbed the counters and then rinsed them with the clean hot water of pure relief.

But from then on Lucky knew how Brigitte would be when she died: just a body without life, not even a flicker of a dream under the eyelids. Deep down, she knew that Brigitte wasn't really safe just because her old mother was still alive. People could die any moment, and when you least expect it.

Of course it wasn't likely that Brigitte would have a fatal accident like Lucky's birth mother, Lucille, who had been electrocuted by a fallen high-tension wire. Brigitte's regular, ho-hum accidents and little colds and minor headaches were okay because that kind of thing wouldn't kill her: Lucky counted on the statistical improbability of any girl having *two* mothers suddenly die from accidents. So she soothed herself out of those death thoughts for a while.

But then they would come back, and Lucky finally had to

make herself envision Brigitte's total death. She ran a little story in her head about the funeral and all the sad French people, Brigitte's sisters and her old mother, coming to Hard Pan and trying to comfort Lucky, but she would not be comforted no matter what they did. In the little story of Brigitte's funeral, Triple T would arrive in his dark glasses, and Lucky would yank those glasses off his face so she could look her father in the eyes. Often the story would end there, because Lucky didn't know where to take it, or she had to give HMS Beagle a bath, or it was time to do her homework, and anyway she'd gotten tired of imagining Brigitte's death.

And Lucky had a secret backup plan in case Brigitte *did* die, because sometimes she needed to calm herself by studying all the possibilities of something bad happening, and what things would occur and what she could do. So her secret plan was that she would make her father take care of her. He didn't want her, which she knew for sure, now that she was eleven and a half and no longer had childish hopes that maybe he just didn't realize how great a daughter he had, that if he got to know her he'd like her very much. No, she was now a total realist as far as her father. He didn't want her: okay.

But she'd make him take her, or at least take care of her so she wouldn't have to go to an orphanage. She knew enough about him to back him up against a wall and say, "Hey! Your parents didn't make *you* go to an orphanage! They sent you to school in Europe! So don't try to weasel out of it with me!" Lucky saw herself as fierce and unyielding, and she saw her father (without his dark glasses) bowing his head.

Plus, *plus*, she thought she could convince Stick to stick up for her. She'd get Stick to get her lawyer to talk to Triple T's lawyer and maybe sue him or something. Couldn't you sue your father for mental anguish if he abandoned you? You *should* be able to, she decided. That was her secret backup plan, how she would handle everything, if Brigitte were to die. She would use the little suitcase that Brigitte brought with her to America, and she would wear her ruby necklace that had been her adopted great-great-grandmother's, and when she arrived at the Paris airport, her aunts (pretty, but not as pretty as Brigitte) would meet her and take her to a fancy French school (*not* an orphanage!) with red geraniums in the windows. In the last scene of this story, Lucky would be looking out the window, down to the street below, and all the women would look just like Brigitte from above, but none of them would be her.

And sometimes she discussed the whole problem with her Higher Power. She always needed to be outdoors to do this, and it was fine for HMS Beagle to be there but no humans. At these times, she'd just have a little conversation with her Higher Power, explaining the situation.

"If Brigitte died," Lucky said aloud to her Higher Power, "I'd just die too. It would be too sad to bear." Lucky cried a little, which she often did during these conversations. "If the Beag died," she went on, "I'd also die from the sadness." She wanted to make it clear to her Higher Power just how much dying she could cope with before it killed her. Sometimes there was an answer, not in an actual voice, but as a sign. This was one of those times. It had been a very still, breezeless morning, like the world was holding its breath. And just then a big billow of warm wind blew right into Lucky's face, the breath of her Higher Power gently blowing out a candle. This, Lucky decided, was a sign. But she wasn't at all sure of what the sign meant.

And there was no one she could ask. She definitely never told anyone about her death thoughts, because she suspected they would make her go to doctors for testing and she'd end up at a school for disturbed children. Well, she was probably a little bit disturbed, but wasn't everybody? And it was not in a bad or alarming way, only inside her own head, where it didn't bother a soul in the world.

So she carefully kept her thoughts to herself, in the privacy of her mind.

Especially her worst thought, a suspicion she was pretty sure about, that no matter how much you try to prepare yourself, no matter how carefully you have thought it all out—what could happen and how you would manage—you can never be ready.

22. safety first

Lucky had collected a large quantity of owl pellets from under one of the Chinese elms behind the old abandoned jail. She wanted to dissect them, so she brought a plastic bag to carry them in and two toothpicks. Since she could never get away with this type of scientific experiment at home because Brigitte wouldn't allow owl pellets in the trailers, Lucky headed to Mrs. Prender's. Justine was pretty cool about Lucky hanging out there, and Miles could play with HMS Beagle. Mrs. Prender herself was at her new job in Sierra City.

That morning Miles had marked off the yard in front of Mrs. Prender's double-wide with a dozen large orange plastic traffic-control cones; it looked as if some major highway construction was going to take place between the unpaved street and the four washing machines lined up on either side of the front door. Miles, wearing Short Sammy's bright orange Adopt-a-Highway vest, was now enthusiastically spearing litter within this coned-off area. He used an official-looking tool with a long pole handle. As Lucky and HMS Beagle approached, the dog ran to Miles and stretched out her front legs, head low, rear end high. Then she leaped straight up in the air.

"It's not a game," Miles said to the Beag, who bowed again and then leaped even higher, all four legs off the ground, like one of those gazelle-type animals on a PBS program. "Explain to her, Lucky. This is official work."

"Sure," Lucky said, and turned to her dog. "Beag, you heard him. Miles isn't playing. The State of California is hiring six-year-olds to stab the litter in their own front yards." Although Lucky said this ironically, HMS Beagle gave it serious consideration, listening with her head cocked to the side. "If you'll check out the traffic cones," Lucky went on, "and the orange vest, you'll notice that this is an official roadwork area." Lucky and Paloma were extremely interested in irony. They agreed that irony was similar to sarcasm, only more mature. Both Lincoln and Miles were becoming accustomed to a lot of irony popping up in everyday conversations.

Miles rolled his eyes. "First, nobody *hires* the Adopt-a-Highway people. They volunteer. I got Short Sammy to lend me his equipment because of too much arguing."

Lucky frowned her eyebrows. "And these orange traffic cones have to do with too much arguing exactly how?"

"Well, last night my grandma told Justine she prayed too much, and Justine told Grandma maybe *she* didn't pray *enough*, and they argued about that, and then they argued about some other things." He stabbed a paper cup with his pole. "I hate it when they argue."

"Let me try that thing," Lucky said. She removed the paper cup, threw it on the ground, and restabbed it. "This is a cool tool." She gave it back to him. "So how did it get from arguing to Adopt-a-Highway in your front yard?"

"Well, I told them about Short Sammy's equipment and asked could I make a special zone here in front if I clean it up, where there's no arguing allowed. And then they stopped arguing and Justine got out her prayer journal and Grandma said it was okay," Miles explained.

Lucky glanced at the front door. A Gatorade bottle, now serving as a hummingbird feeder, hung upside down from the porch ceiling. "So they'll still argue inside, but if you get sick of it you can come out here and stab litter. Good plan." Miles peered at her for traces of irony. She sighed and ruffled his thick, coppery hair and said, "Well, for Pete's sake, throw a stick or something. HMS Beagle thinks the cones and the vest and the pole are some kind of game and that you've been hoping she'll come and play with you." She turned back to her dog, leaning forward to put her hands on her knees, and slapped her palms on her thighs. HMS Beagle understood. She ran in a circle and leaped in the air.

Miles grinned, placed his pole to the side, and looked around the yard, which was nearly free of litter but still contained a wealth of discarded but potentially useful stuff. He spotted an ancient, rotting tennis ball, coming apart at the seams and encrusted with layers of dirt and grit, but still a ball. HMS Beagle, who was watching him because she understood that he was ready to play, also saw the ball and knew what it was for. It was a thing for throwing, and it smelled of rabbit urine and the rubber of a car tire that had run over it, and it smelled of Miles, who had picked it up earlier and then dropped it back onto the ground because it was still too good to get rid of. The Beag knew he would throw it as far as he could and she would bring it back. She was outstanding at this game. She turned her body in readiness to fly after the ball, never taking her eyes off Miles's hand. He raised his arm and sailed the ball out toward the faraway Coso Range. The dog was after it in a blur and returned a few seconds later, dropping it at Miles's feet, waiting for him to throw it again.

Lucky moved toward the front door as Miles praised the Beag and made several feints with the ball, pretending to throw it. HMS remained alert but lowered her rear to the ground to show she knew this was part of the game; she could wait. Lucky gave two short raps on the door, called out "Justine?" and eased the door open slightly, waiting to be invited inside. This was good visiting manners in Hard Pan. She turned back around to say, "Hey, I'm dissecting some owl pellets inside. You can watch if you want."

Miles shook his head and turned back to HMS Beagle. He'd seen plenty of owl pellets, and he had a pretty good idea Justine would not like them one bit. "We're fine out here, aren't we, Beag?" he said.

HMS Beagle crowded up close to Miles so he would scratch her right between her shoulders, in the place she couldn't reach herself. He did, and the Beag noted that he smelled of many things: of himself most strongly, of ball, of Short Sammy, of cookies, and of Lucky. He smelled, in other words, exactly right.

23. MUCUS

"Back here," Justine called, and Lucky walked through a curtain of walnut shells that clicked and clacked against one another like a kind of musical instrument. Justine had made it by drilling tiny holes in the tops and bottoms of each half shell and threading them with lengths of dental floss. These long ropes of shells were then tied close together onto a pole across the top of the door frame. She said they acted like a screen, keeping flies away, and also helped her keep track of Miles as he ran in and out of the house. Everyone in town wanted her to make *them* a walnut-shell curtain, but Justine had run out of shells, and besides, she said she wanted a new project.

Lucky found her on the floor of the kitchen, locked in battle with a wire coat hanger, as if she wanted to maim it badly before putting it to death. "Hey," Lucky said as she sat, cross-legged, on the beat-up linoleum.

There were three main aspects about Justine that Lucky

had observed. One: She was very, very religious, but without being all holy or saintly about it; two: She always seemed nervous or worried; and three: She liked to make things out of stuff people threw away. Like the walnut-shell curtain and the hummingbird feeder, and probably, Lucky guessed, whatever this wire hanger was being made into.

Fortunately, Justine was also beginning to pick up some basic mom-skills. Lucky knew for a fact that she made excellent hot dogs (the exact proportion of ketchup and mayo and mustard and chopped onions and sweet pickles) and great tuna melts and also perfect mac and cheese and a good PB&J sandwich. A strong, reliable, and good-tasting repertory. Lucky was used to Brigitte's unstoppable interest in food, every kind of food and every way to prepare it and season it and serve it, and how to store it and preserve it and when to get more of it. So it was kind of restful to be around a mom who wasn't constantly experimenting with strange ingredients and who didn't talk about food all the time.

The tradeoff was hearing a lot of stuff from the Bible. To Justine, every single thing in the world had a connection to the Bible. It was her rule book. Ask a question about anything and she could find the answer, or something that she could interpret as an answer, in her Bible. It was interesting as long as she didn't go too far overboard.

As Miles's almost-big-sister, Lucky felt it her duty to be available in case Justine needed tips, pointers, or the benefit of her wisdom in terms of motherhood decisions, just as she had helped Brigitte in *her* beginning-mom period. Lucky was very generous with her advice. So she hung out at the Prenders' every so often when Mrs. Prender herself was at her cashier job at the Buy-Mor-Store in Sierra City. (Justine had been the one who wanted a job, but she didn't have a driver's license or a car, so instead her mother, Mrs. Prender, got hired and drove into town four days a week.)

After watching Justine's fierce assault on the hanger for a few more minutes, Lucky asked, "Um, Justine, what's up with the coat hanger?"

"I need pliers to bend this thing. Where do you think she keeps them?"

140

"Probably in the jar-lid drawer," Lucky said. "Wait a sec." She found the tool and handed it over to Justine. Then she pulled an old newspaper off a stack in the corner and spread it on the floor, dumping the plastic bag full of owl pellets on top.

"I'm trying"—Justine broke off as she struggled to bend the curved hook at the top of the hanger back and downward—"to rig up a book-holder. So I can prop a book open while I work. I have to make Miles's lunches."

Lucky had noticed a row of bread slices on the kitchen counter; it looked like the whole loaf. "What, you make more than one day's lunch at a time?"

Justine clamped the pliers onto one foot of the wire triangle's base. With a mighty effort she bent it forward, forming a little corner. "It's a time-saving technique," she explained to Lucky. "You make five lunches at a time and then it's all done and ready in the morning and you're not all frantic, flying around to find the peanut butter and making Miles miss his bus."

"Wow," Lucky said admiringly, although the white bread was already drying out. Everything dried out—apples, bread, salt, even things you don't think of as *having* humidity, like newspapers and wooden salad bowls—just by being exposed to the Hard Pan air, which sucked up moisture like Miles sucked up chocolate milk with a straw. Even the stuff in your nose—mucus, one of those words Lucky loved because it sounded medical and much more scientific than "snot"—dried out. It got so dried out that it became like little rocks stuck in your nostrils. Lucky had observed, without people realizing it, that everyone in Hard Pan picked their noses at some time or other to get rid of that dried-out mucus.

But Short Sammy had once pointed out to Lucky that sometimes scientists make observations without *necessarily* expressing *all* of them *aloud*. So she did not share with Justine either her mucus thoughts or her dried-out-bread thoughts. She had learned that living in Hard Pan sometimes meant dried sandwiches, and there are worse things in the world.

Justine nudged a stack of small brown paper bags that had had previous uses but were now flattened out as much as crumpled brown bags *can* be flattened out. "You just do an assembly-line kind of thing, get everything organized. You mark your little lunch bags with his name." She bent the opposite side of the hanger, making another corner so that the two ends of the base of the wire triangle curved forward and the top hook was twisted back. She set it on the floor and carefully placed her open Bible into its grasp. The book stayed open and propped up at a perfect angle for reading.

"That's extremely cool, Justine," Lucky said, "being able to read and make peanut butter sandwiches at the same—"

"Ew!" Justine said. She had just noticed Lucky's pile of brownish gray, furry-looking ovals, each about an inch long—owl pellets. "What *are* those?" She scooched away from the newspaper and snatched the Bible from its holder and clutched it to her chest, wrapped in her arms, as if the pellets, just lying there, could contaminate it. She leaned her head on her knees, one heel beating a fast rhythm on the floor, and took deep breaths. Then she looked piercingly at Lucky, waiting.

Lucky frowned at her. "Justine, these are owl pellets! It's, like, fur and bones and teeth and other stuff that owls can't digest."

"But why would *you* want those things? Why did you dump them *here*?" She pointed to the kitchen floor. "That is the most disgusting thing I've ever seen. Gah!"

"Hang on, Justine. Check this out." Lucky got out her two toothpicks. "So what they do, the owls—and these are the small ones you see about a half hour after the sun sets—is they eat a mouse or a little bird or a wood rat. But—think about it—owls don't have teeth!" Lucky loved this part. It was such a clever way for owls to have adapted to not being able to chew. "So they swallow everything whole or in big chunks and it all gets sorted out in their stomach. In a thing called a gizzard. Then after a while, they regurgitate these pellets, the stuff they couldn't digest."

Justine's already high-pitched voice got even higher. "When do we find out what *you're* doing with them, and why you're doing it on this kitchen floor?"

"Okay, wait. Don't freak out." Lucky gently pulled a pellet apart with her toothpicks. It was dry and not too dense, and there was a mild, not unpleasant musky smell. Inside the pellet were the perfectly clean white bones of a tiny creature. She put these aside in a little pile, then started on another pellet with her toothpicks.

Justine gaped at the tiny, delicate bones. "Wash your hands before you touch anything," she said, but she sounded different, not so disgusted. She leaned forward to look at the bones

more closely. "What kind of animal are they from? These look just like human leg bones. Whoa—that's a skull."

"I think it's a little mouse, or part of one," Lucky said. "It's not a bird, because this stuff is fur, not feathers."

Justine carefully picked up one of the bones. It was half the length of a toothpick and intricately shaped. "Incredible," she said.

Lucky frowned. As a scientist, she loved studying the pellets. But Justine seemed fascinated for some other reason. She'd gone from totally repulsed to totally interested in three seconds. What was up with that?

"Can you take all the bones out of those pellets and give them to me? Can you get more?" Justine was now arranging the bones on the palm of her hand, lining them up. Lucky stared at her. "I can't get over how perfect they are," Justine continued. "Very light, but strong."

"Hey, wash your hands before you touch anything," Lucky said, feeling half-ironic and half-crabby. "Why should I give you my owl pellets?"

"I don't want the whole thing. Yuck. Just the bones inside them."

Lucky couldn't figure what the deal was with the bones. "But what for?" she said.

Justine was rearranging the skull and the pelvis; she

seemed to be concentrating. "I need them, Lucky," she said, not exactly answering the question. "All that you can find. I'll owe you. I don't have any money, but we can figure out some other way I can pay you back. I could make you something. Please." She looked like a kid begging for a pair of red leather cowboy boots—something she wanted *bad*. And this appealed strongly to Lucky.

Maybe owl pellets would be a really big point in Hard Pan's favor if Justine was ever thinking of moving away with Miles— like if she wanted to live in a town where there was a church. If owl pellets meant Miles could stay, Lucky would gather them forever. And providing the stuff would be easy: She knew the particular branch of the Chinese elm where a couple of owls always went to regurgitate their pellets—she could get, maybe, eight of them every day at the same place.

"Well," Lucky said. "Okay, I guess. But you have to tell me why you want them."

"Next time, when you bring more. Leave me everything you have there, and when you come by tomorrow afternoon you'll see."

So Lucky set to work separating the bones from the other material in the pellets, and Justine aligned them in various patterns. For once, the Bible lay, along with its coat-hanger holder, off to the side, unread.

Before she left, Lucky washed her hands and helped Justine finish making the sandwiches. Remembering a tip from Short

Sammy, she dropped a piece of peeled carrot inside each little plastic Ziploc sandwich bag, to give the bread something with moisture that *it* could suck up.

As they worked, her radio playing rock-and-roll music in the background, Justine studied her pile of tiny bones again and again. When they finished making the sandwiches, she pulled Lucky's hands together and clutched them tightly in her own, their four hands a ball that Justine tucked for a moment under her chin. It was a little odd and but also cool, having her hands captured like that, as if they were precious to Justine, and Lucky didn't try to take them back.

146

24. getting into heaven

"I've got fifteen pellets," Lucky said to Justine the next day. "I found another place where owls regurgitate them."

Justine had newspaper already spread out on the table. Lucky admired her gelled, spiked-up hair, which was the same coppery color as Miles's but a shade darker. It was certainly very *convenient* hair because it never got in your way and could be washed in about one second and required no barrettes or scrunchies. "Fantastic! Oh, this is great, Lucky, the more the better. I'll help you get the bones out if you want me to," she offered, but Lucky could tell she didn't really want to.

In fact, Lucky enjoyed dissecting them herself. "It's okay," she said as she dumped the pellets onto the newspaper. "So Miles is still doing his Adopt-a-Yard thing again today. The Beag thinks the vest and the special equipment mean it's some kind of game. She gets really excited when she sees him like that."

"We got into another fight this morning when I wouldn't let him wear the vest to school."

"Yeah, he told me on the bus. He was talking about hell again. I don't know what to tell him when he asks me questions about it. Maybe it's against your religion or something for me to say this, but I, like, usually don't go around all the time thinking about hell, or at least not that *often*. So he asks me stuff and I'm, like, '*I* don't know, Miles.'"

Today Justine sat at the breakfast table like a normal mom, instead of on the floor. Well, her collection of Popsicle sticks, a cereal box full of them, was maybe a little unusual, but not in the sense of *ab*normal. She was just different. "Lucky, it's simple and easy. You need to believe that Jesus came to die for your sins, and you ask Him to forgive you. That's how you go to heaven instead of hell. Hand me that glue." Her fingers, with their tiny nails, looked like they belonged to a young girl; Lucky liked watching because they were very precise, skillful fingers. They were fingers that knew exactly what they were doing. She spread white glue on the ends of several Popsicle sticks and began arranging them in stacks. "And if Miles asks questions you don't know the answers to, just tell him to come to me. You too, Lucky. You know you should feel free to ask me questions anytime."

"Well," Lucky said hesitantly. "Okay. Here's one thing I was wondering about—it's about after I die, if I go to heaven, would I get to meet Charles Darwin in person? Because he was this very, very great scientist and he was kind of spiritual, almost like he thought every single living thing had God inside it. And in this book I'm reading it says he and his wife had different religious beliefs. *She* was pretty religious, but I don't know if Darwin actually believed what you said. You know, that Jesus died for his sins. So, does that mean he wouldn't be able to go to heaven?" Lucky considered meeting Charles Darwin as a huge bonus, in terms of being dead.

"Especially not him," Justine said, shaking her head.

This felt the same as when someone shoves their knees into the backs of yours and makes them buckle. It doesn't hurt, but it's annoying because it takes you unfairly by surprise. "Why *especially* not him?" she demanded, tearing a pellet apart with her toothpicks.

"Evolution," Justine said. "What Charles Darwin came up with. It's a lie, Lucky. He sinned, just like we all do, and I guess it's like any other sin to God, but to me his sin was compounded because so many people have been turned away from God by his theories."

Lucky watched Justine's small fingers carefully stack the Popsicle sticks, squaring them before the glue could dry; alternating the arrangement so that the sticks supported each other and began to form a smooth strong surface about a foot square. This was going to be the base for the pellet bone project, apparently. "But they teach us about evolution in *school*. We have *textbooks*. Everyone knows Charles Darwin was the greatest scientist who ever lived." Lucky hoped that by explaining these things to Justine, she would realize that maybe she needed to relook at the whole getting-into-heaven criteria.

Justine shook her head at Lucky. "I didn't make the rules," she said. "It's all in there." She pointed the bottle of glue at her Bible. "This is the word of God and it's all we have to go on. But once you take Jesus into your heart, you'll be saved. 'Every good gift and every perfect gift is from above, and comes down from the Father of lights, with whom there is no variation or shadow of turning.' Think about that passage, Lucky, from the book of James. You'll see that it's comforting."

Lucky still hadn't gotten over Charles Darwin being denied entrance into heaven, like a goof-off kid held back at the entrance to Disneyland. Charles Darwin should be in *charge* of heaven! Then Lucky had another thought. "Pete's a Christian, but he's also a geologist and he believes in evolution. And what about people who maybe grew up studying another religion completely, where they don't even have Jesus? Or they have their own sacred book, not our Bible, but just as holy to them. Can't any of those people go to heaven either?

"And what about me?" Lucky kept finding questions, like the tiny bones in the pellets. "If I have a good heart, I'm kind, I don't cheat, I 'do unto others,' I'm not evil or bad." In fact, deep down, Lucky knew that she was *not* very good. She could be mean and sometimes she didn't recycle or she left lights on and used up energy unnecessarily. Paloma was much better at stuff like not harming the Earth; she was a truly good person, whereas Lucky herself had many faults. And sometimes very bad thoughts. But she figured that hypothetically by the time she died (of old age) she'd be making better choices and decisions. And that meant that God or whoever was in charge of the universe would very, very likely welcome her into heaven. And Charles Darwin, too!

Justine, wiping off some extra globs of glue with a piece of toilet paper, said, "You want to know if you can be saved and live with Christ in heaven by doing good?"

"Yeah," Lucky said. "Wouldn't God be okay with me, even if I'd never read a page of the Bible? Or if I belonged to another religion?"

"No, Lucky. There is only one door into heaven," Justine said. Standing, she gave Lucky the exact same imploring look as HMS Beagle when she had an urgent need—to eat or to play or to go out. After a second, Justine turned to the counter behind her; she punched on the radio and pulled an iron out of a cupboard. "I want so much for you to go through that door, for you to be saved." She placed the iron on the Popsicle stick platform and left it there; Lucky saw that it would weigh down the structure while it was drying.

Lucky had heard the song on Justine's Christian station before—it was a sweet ballad. She half listened to it, thinking about two things she longed and longed and longed to talk with Charles Darwin about. One was the death of his daughter, Annie, at the age of ten. Lucky wanted Charles Darwin to know how sad she felt about that, and how she planned to name her own daughter Annie Darwin. And she also wanted to tell him about certain coincidences, such as how she and Charles had both been eight when their mothers died, and that Charles was born on the exact same day and year as Abraham Lincoln, for whom her friend Lincoln was named; Lucky found these to be *extraordinary* coincidences, and proof of some kind of spiritual connection between them.

Lucky decided to discuss questions about heaven and hell more thoroughly with Lincoln at some point. Which reminded her: "I hope," she said, "that Klincke Ken will remember to use Lincoln's latch, that little noose he made, to keep his new gate closed. Otherwise Chesterfield is going to keep wandering around town and getting into trouble and dangerous situations like on cabin-moving day. He might even leave completely and go find his old burro buds in the desert. Miles loves Chesterfield so much I think that would just about kill him."

Tapping a Popsicle stick against the table in time to the music, Justine said, "My guess is, if that burro wants to get out, he'll get out. If he feels like he's locked up, no little noose latch is going to stop him. But if he *decides* to stick around, if he's given up the wild life he had before, well . . . and I heard about how much he loves that little ginger cat. Is that true?"

Lucky smiled. "Lincoln and I were watching them together the other day, and it sounds crazy because they're different species and everything, but it's like they really need each other."

"Then Klincke Ken probably doesn't even have to use the latch."

Lucky had a feeling Justine was right about that, even if she was wrong about other things. She said, "I like that song a lot. So, listen, you promised to tell me what the owl pellet bones are for."

"A sculpture!" Justine said, like someone calling out, "Cold watermelon!" on a hot day. She sang along with the chorus, "'He's right here in this room, the helper of the fatherless, a father of the fatherless . . .'"

"A sculpture? You mean like a marble statue with no arms?" Lucky had seen one like this in Dot's backyard, which she'd gotten cheap at the garden supply store because it had a little crack in it. Dot said her statue gave the place a very classical aspect that appealed to her beauty parlor customers. But Lucky didn't see the connection between a statue like that and rodent bones. "I don't think these bones will work, Justine," she said.

153

Justine laughed. "No, not a statue of a person. It's going to be a staircase, a miniature staircase, one with a handrail, built entirely of these tiny bones. I'll need hundreds and hundreds more of them."

"Okay," Lucky said. She tried picturing Justine's sculpture, but it was too strange to imagine. "Um, but who is the staircase for? Why are you making it?"

"Because I have to. I can't really explain. I see it in my mind and I have to make it."

Lucky said nothing. She gently stirred the box of bones with a finger, thinking of the words of the song, how God was the father of the fatherless. She wondered whether God knew about that time she had that what-if thought, *What if Brigitte's Hard Pan Café suddenly disappeared?* But if her Higher Power did hear what-ifs, she hoped he'd know that they were *not* little unintentional prayers. Mostly what-ifs are hopes or anxiousness or even bad thoughts that need to be gone over by a person privately. Lucky's what-ifs were extremely personal, none of anyone's business, even her Higher Power's. Anyway, she reasoned, a Higher Power has much more important things to do than pay attention to those questions in her head.

25. saving on kleenex

The walnut shells rattled and Mrs. Prender shouted, "Justine? Give me a hand with these bags?"

Lucky and Justine jumped up to relieve Mrs. Prender of two big grocery bags from the Buy-Mor-Store. Mrs. Prender sank onto a chair as Miles wandered into the kitchen and opened the fridge door. "Long day," Mrs. Prender said. She always spoke very loudly, and Lucky used to think this was because she herself might be hard of hearing. But Mrs. Prender always heard every word Lucky said, even whispered words, so Lucky concluded that Mrs. Prender, for whatever reason, set her personal voice volume louder than most people.

"Miles, get out of the fridge, please," Justine said.

Miles grabbed a handful of grapes from a bowl, stuffed them in his mouth, and slammed the fridge door. He turned to his mother and stood in front of her, chewing the grapes, opening his mouth wide with each chew.

"Quit that, Miles!" shouted Mrs. Prender. "Why is he always acting up the minute I come home?"

"He's like that all the time," Justine said.

"No, he's not," Lucky put in. "He's only been like that since—" She stopped. It would have been rude to say the truth: He'd only been like that since Justine arrived in Hard Pan.

Miles pawed around in the grocery bags, then went to sit next to Lucky on the kitchen chair, pushing her so that each of them had half the seat. She let him, even though there was an empty chair next to them.

"I brought you some books from the Sierra City Library," Mrs. Prender told Miles. "The librarian helped me pick them out. She knows you've read most of what they've got for your age group and she thought you'd like these. They're out in the car—backseat."

Miles jumped up and shot through the walnut shell curtain. In a minute he shot back through and flung a pile of books onto the kitchen table.

"I have to look at those first, Miles," Justine said.

"Awww, Justine!" Miles said.

"Miles . . . you know the drill." Justine gave him a look.

Miles sighed and told Lucky, "She needs to make sure they're appropriate. Dinosaur books aren't appropriate. I can't read those anymore. Some geology books are bad because they say the Earth is much older than it really is. Like I had a book about the Grand Canyon, but we had to return it because it said the canyon was formed, well, parts of it, two billion years ago. That's wrong. I can read about the human body as long as it doesn't talk about you-know-what." Miles had an innocent, open way of explaining all this, but Lucky knew him as if he were her brother. Even though Miles hated it when his mother and grandmother argued, she could tell he was trying to get his grandmother, who'd raised him and had always let him read everything, to start an argument with Justine.

And sure enough, Mrs. Prender started in. "Justine, reading isn't going to make Miles into a sinner. He's already read more books than I read in my whole life. They said he's a genius at the school there in Sierra City. You really think God would give him such a good brain and then not want him to use it?"

"Mom, please stop. We've been over this. He's my kid, and I don't want him reading books that go against anything God teaches us."

"Well, he's your kid, but since I raised him so far, he's also my kid. So what I'm saying," Mrs. Prender shouted, "is give him some slack. I'm sick of this and I'm too old for it."

Justine had been facing the sink, her spiky boy-haircut bowed, and Lucky wondered how much the tattooed cross on the back of her neck had hurt. Then Justine turned around, her face covered with tears, looking to Lucky so young that she could have been a student at Einstein Junior High. "Well, I am sick of it too!" she said. "You don't get it! If it weren't for God, I'd be a drug addict and I'd probably be on the streets. He saved my body and He saved my soul in prison. You can't understand that, but that's what guides my life now."

Lucky actually did understand, because she had eavesdropped at twelve-step meetings when she was younger. The meetings were a way for people to stop being addicted by doing a fearless and searching moral inventory and being honest and asking forgiveness of those they did harm to. There were more steps, but that was the gist of it that Lucky remembered. Also she knew that Mrs. Prender attended those meetings as a recovering smoker. By eavesdropping, Lucky had learned all about what it was like for people to hit rock bottom because of their addictions, and then find their Higher Power and get well. God was Justine's Higher Power.

But at the anonymous meetings there was no particular God everyone had to agree on—you could be any religion or no religion and just have a personal Higher Power, like Lucky did herself, without the Bible or a church. She remembered one man who wasn't from Hard Pan. He used to show up for the Gamblers Anonymous meetings, and before the prayer at the end he would always say, "Oh God of our many understandings," and Lucky would sometimes think of that phrase because it was so beautiful and mysterious. In some ways, eavesdropping on those meetings was like going to a sort of unofficial do-it-yourself church.

"Miles," Justine said, her tears gone, "I need to study the *California Driver Handbook*. Want to help? You can test me on the rules."

Miles had begun to cry when his mother did, but now he pulled up the front of his T-shirt and wiped his eyes and nose with it before following her out of the room.

"You must save a lot on Kleenex," Lucky said to Mrs. Prender.

"Yes, and he's also a walking napkin," Mrs. Prender agreed. She heaved herself out of the chair and began to put away the groceries. Lucky gathered up her nondissected pellets and cleaned up the area where she'd been working. It hit her—how Justine's new life in Hard Pan was hard for her and hard in a different way for Miles, but it was maybe even hardest of all for Mrs. Prender. She wanted to explain that she kind of understood; she wanted to say the right thing but didn't know how, so instead she said very softly, "They'll be okay."

"God willing," Mrs. Prender answered, and for once her voice was soft too. She pulled a tiny plastic pot from the grocery bag and handed it to Lucky. "Here, these rosemary seedlings were on sale. I got one for Brigitte."

Lucky looked at it worriedly. The little plant was so straggly she wondered if it would ever grow. Mrs. Prender noticed and smiled. "Don't worry," she said. "It's hardier than you think."

159

26. small talk

Lincoln and his parents would be leaving Hard Pan tomorrow at four a.m., driving to the airport in Los Angeles for an early flight to London. Lucky had gone over to the Kennedys' after dinner to say good-bye, but there were a lot of other people milling around, and suddenly Lucky felt something in her chest like a black hole in space, and it seemed it was going to suck her into itself. The feeling made her give up trying to say just the right thing to Lincoln, the exact perfect words so he would know how much she was going to miss him.

What people do, when a lot of folks are all talking and getting together for some special event, is they make small talk. Lucky found this a good description: small talk, where nothing much is said. It must be so restful to be some other kind of animal, she thought. You could hang out with your friends and no chatter or small talk would be necessary: You could nuzzle them, or you could let them lick your ears, or you could swim along beside them—but you didn't have to think of anything to say.

Short Sammy was explaining to Lincoln about the rate of exchange between dollars and English pounds, and Klincke Ken wondered if the wrist brace, with its metal splint, would set off the airport security alarms, and everybody admired Lincoln's new leather jacket, excited to be sending him off on his big adventure. If only Paloma were there, Lucky would say, "Let me introduce you to Betty Lou, Mrs. Kennedy's sofa," and she knew Paloma would explode with laughter, and then people would want to know why they were laughing so hard, and Paloma would explain in that way she had that always made other people laugh too, even grown-ups.

And then she and Paloma and Lincoln would escape out the back and make normal talk. Lincoln, being Lincoln, would get them thinking about poor Stu Burping having to endure a lifetime of people laughing at his name, and Lincoln would mention how he himself being named for four presidents wasn't always a picnic either. And Lucky would feel again that amazement at Lincoln's friendship. No matter how mean she was, like laughing at Stu Burping's name, he never criticized her and always liked her.

But Lucky couldn't handle the small talk when what she needed was big talk. She needed to say important things but couldn't, so she made her way through the crowd to the door. Then she turned back, hesitating, and found Lincoln looking

161

at her intently, as if he were trying to communicate something across the room through ESP. She waved and smiled, and in a sudden impulse, she blew him a kiss, like a movie star of the olden days. The theatrical gesture was supposed to be ironic, as if to say *of course* she would miss him a *little* but the time would absolutely *zip* by because they would both be having so much fun!

When you spend your entire childhood with someone, there are certain things you can do impulsively, like blowing kisses, which you would *never* do with some boy you knew from school, who would misinterpret and think you were doing it because you were madly in love with him. Lucky was confident that Lincoln would understand exactly, and would know it was just a movie-star pantomime to make him laugh.

But he nodded at her, very serious. As Klincke Ken and Short Sammy flipped a coin, settling some dispute, Lincoln brought his hands together, making a gesture low to his waist. It was a private, brief hand sign that no one saw but Lucky, his fingertips pointing down and touching in a V shape, and his thumbnails pressed together back-to-back. Then Lucky got the hidden meaning, not in Lincoln's fingers but in the shape created by them: a heart. She smiled at him: *Yes*. And she slipped out, closing the door quietly.

"Look," Lucky said in a low voice to HMS Beagle later, when Brigitte had gone to bed. "It's not a big thing." HMS Beagle looked up from her rug on the floor by Lucky's bed. Lucky stared back. "What," she said, "you think he was sending some kind of love message? Oh, please. We were both just joking around." HMS Beagle sighed, and then put her head down between her paws.

But even though she said that to her dog, Lucky felt some deep pressure around her, like being inside a tube of toothpaste while someone squeezed it. She put on her old sleeveless summer nightie and turned off the light.

Lucky woke up deep in the night, when it feels as if the world is breathing more slowly and the nocturnal creatures come out to have their day.

She went from deeply asleep to fully awake; she lay still, listening, trying to figure out what woke her. HMS Beagle raised her head from the rug, looked at Lucky, and then scrambled to her feet, smelling at the crack at the foot of the door.

Lucky followed. Holding the Beag's collar, she opened the door.

It was Lincoln.

"Hey," he whispered. "Can you come out a minute?"

He was wearing jeans and his new leather jacket, soft brown suede; it made him look cool and tough and handsome and grown-up, like a person who could figure his way around an airport or actually ask someone out on a date. Lucky felt like a little girl in her faded nightgown. "What time is it?" she asked.

"Two thirty," Lincoln said. "I snuck out."

Lucky nodded. The night was moonless and dark, but there were stars enough to see by. Moths fluttered, a bat swooped around, and the crickets made a racket. She leaned against the aluminum side of her canned-ham trailer bedroom. "This'll be good," she said, meaning the whole trip to London, the chance to tie knots with Geoffrey Budworth, work on *Knotting Matters*.

"Yeah. It'll go fast. Next time we see each other, in a couple of months, you'll be eleven and—" Lincoln took Lucky's hand and put some coins in her palm. "Eleven and—"

She looked at the coins. "Three quarters," she finished, grinning. "Right."

Lincoln swung his sprained arm a little.

"Isn't your wrist getting better? I bet it didn't help when you jumped up onto Klincke Ken's loader."

"If all of you children," he said in a perfect imitation of Dr. Strictmund, sounding exactly like a principal, "had stayed behind Short Sammy's orange traffic cones, none of this would have happened." In his normal voice Lincoln went on, "No, it's better." He wiggled his fingers to show that he could. "Ollie turns out to be okay, you know?"

"Yeah . . . I think he has a thing for Brigitte."

"Who doesn't?"

Lucky laughed. "My mom, the heartthrob."

"What I'll really miss—" Lincoln broke off as HMS Beagle came to stand next to him, pressing her body sideways against his legs. Lucky saw this and knew that the Beag was responding to strong feelings from Lincoln. It was the comforting thing HMS Beagle did when Lucky felt sadness or yearning or longing—sometimes she didn't even know for what. Lincoln stroked the Beag with his uninjured left hand. "Yes, girl, I'll miss you."

Lucky wondered what Lincoln had been about to say. She clutched the three quarters as if it were her fare for a special kind of ride that she was about to go on. An owl called out, a series of short single hoots, and she thought of all the pellets she'd dissected. "Lincoln," she said finally, "do you think I'll go to hell when I die?"

He laughed. "If you do, I'm going too, because who wants to go to heaven if they won't admit you?"

"No, I'm serious."

"So am I," he said. "Jeez, Lucky, maybe heaven and hell are happening right now. You know what I mean?"

"No." But she did, sort of.

"Maybe it's not what happens after we die. Maybe heaven and hell are when we're alive, and we get some of both during our lifetime. But it's the way we see all the things that happen to us, I guess, and the choices we make. Did Short Sammy ever tell you that old chopsticks story about it?"

She shook her head. In the dark, her hair was like dandelion fluff, reflecting starlight, floating around her head as if it would blow away with the slightest breeze. A zinging sensation shot through her as Lincoln touched her hair with his fingertips.

166   "Well," he said, "I've heard him tell it a bunch of times. There's a Chinese man who wants to find out what heaven and hell are like, and he gets the chance to check them out. First he goes to this place where the tables are covered with food, really good stuff, but everyone's starving and miserable because their chopsticks are three feet long—they can't get the food into their mouths. That was hell. Then he goes to another place and it's exactly the same: lots of food on the tables; again the chopsticks are three feet long. But here everyone is happy and feasting, because they're feeding each other across the table. That was heaven."

HMS Beagle remained pressed against Lincoln during this story. She seemed to sense that he had a powerful wistfulness or eagerness, some strong wanting of something, and she tried to give comfort with her body.

"She can tell that my stomach is full of knots," Lincoln said. He laughed. "You'd think I could handle knots by now."

They both leaned in to touch the dog; Lincoln smelled like leather and spicy hair gel and a sharp scent Lucky couldn't name—she guessed maybe it was the smell of adventure. "Well," she said reluctantly, "you should go home before they start looking, and I should go inside. The Beag can't figure out what's going on. To her it's like, why are we out here in the middle of the night?"

"She doesn't know if she's in heaven or hell, I guess."

"Me either," Lucky said. "And I can't find my chopsticks anywhere."

"Actually, we don't need them," Lincoln said, and put his arms around her. For a long moment, before he jogged away into the night, she could feel his smile at the sweet curling edge of their kiss.

27. a heart problem

Your father has been very ill.

[Stick e-mailed]

He asked me to come here to San Francisco. I did because he said he wanted to finally settle our differences, the two of us, no lawyers.

He had had heart surgery and was in the hospital when I arrived.

We did settle matters between us, a very great weight off my mind. But mainly what I want to say is that I told him you got in touch with me and we had been e-mailing. I told him about your wanting to be a scientist like Charles Darwin.

Taggart is scheduled for more surgery tomorrow, and the doctors are guardedly optimistic. I'll keep you posted.

—Stick

That afternoon, perhaps because she'd been up the night before, Lucky fell asleep while reading on her bed. She dreamed she was in some kind of a ward, confined to her bed, and Lincoln brought her a small red bowl filled with soup. It smelled like wontons.

"Is it Chinese?" Lucky asked.

"It's Forgiveness-Flower soup," Lincoln said. "You don't need chopsticks. Just slurp it." He grinned at her. "It's good, *and* it's good *for* you!" He sounded like a TV commercial. He had braces on both his wrists, and suddenly there was a *naaaat, naaaat* sound of buzzers going off.

"I set off the security sensors with the metal splints in my bandages," he said, winking at her. "But don't be alarmed. Get it? Don't be *alarmed*, Lucky."

When she woke a short time later, Lucky lay in bed wishing Lincoln were there. She didn't remember anything about her dream except that he had been in it. Then she sensed something, and it was odd because it had never happened before inside her canned-ham trailer. It was her Higher Power.

It filled up the trailer like a swirl of warm afternoon air, and it made her feel weightless and serene, like when she went out in the desert to think about things when no one was around.

Suddenly she remembered her father in the hospital. Tears came to her eyes, as they always used to do when she thought of him; when she wanted him in her life even though he was a dreadful person and a terrible father. Now a strange new feeling poured through her.

For the first time she thought of Tag not as her father but just as a person. He had lost his mother to illness, he'd lost his half sister to a long, long argument, he'd lost both his wives. So he must have thought, okay, that's it, no kids; not taking any more chances, not with *this* heart. Usually she'd be angry, thinking these thoughts about how he didn't want children, but now she understood that for his whole life his heart was just a poor battered tender aching thing that hurt and hurt and hurt. How could any heart keep on beating with so much pain in it?

She felt sorry that she could not comfort him. Her Higher Power surrounded her, a kind, understanding, immense presence.

Lucky closed her eyes. She was filled with grace and encircled by it. Her own heart felt large and strong, and with it she forgave her father. An hour later she received another e-mail from Stick.

> I am so sorry, Lucky, dear. Your father died this morning, a few minutes ago. His heart could not be repaired.
>
> Taggart didn't want any services. I shall respect his wishes and take care of everything here.
>
> He left instructions for me regarding something he wants me to send to you. More on this later.
>
> I know that he loved you in his own way.
>
> —Stick

28. no matter what it is, it won't be right

Once the school year was over everything seemed suspended, as if, Lucky thought, time itself waited to find out what was going to happen.

Lucky missed Lincoln. She missed Miles, who spent a lot of time studying the Bible. She missed Paloma between the as-often-as-possible weekend visits. In a strange way, she even missed her father. It was because of the strong, pounding fact that he was no longer on the Earth; he was gone. It took her a long time to realize the true meaning: that she would never see him again, ever.

Then two packages, postmarked San Francisco, arrived for her. On the return label was scrawled TTT C/O S. T. KELLY with Stick's Portland address.

Apart from a monthly bank notification for Brigitte that an automatic deposit had been transferred to her account from Triple T's account, these boxes were the only thing that had ever come from her father, even though it was Stick who had actually mailed them after he died.

Lucky stared at the boxes, hesitating. They were big enough for a large microwave oven to fit inside, and extremely heavy. She wanted to tear into them, find out what he had sent. At the same time, she feared that whatever it was would be wrong: too young for her, or too old, too cheap or too expensive, too not-what-she-wanted-or-needed, too clearly a thing from a stranger to a stranger, too late and too little. She didn't want this gift, this offering, to change the way she thought about him, which was that he was a sad man who died of a bad heart. Even though she had forgiven him, she was afraid. Because why had both Lucille, Lucky's first mother, and also Brigitte, her adopted mother, why had they loved him and married him? If she learned the answer, was there danger that Lucky would love him too?

Lucky did not want to love her father, especially now that he was dead.

She left the packages on the Formica table all afternoon. Sometimes she glanced at them or frowned at them. Part of her wanted to throw them, unopened, in the trash, but another part of her, the part that won, needed to see what he possibly could have sent: what he imagined she would want, what kind of person he believed her to be, what he wanted her to understand about him. Finally she gave up and went to the everything drawer for the scissors.

She slid one scissor blade along the tape, that bright shiny wide sticky tape that cannot be torn but is easily cut.

A surge of disappointment washed through Lucky. The boxes were both filled with books—adult books that looked dull and difficult. In one box there was a sealed envelope marked "From Stick to Lucky."

She opened it.

Dear Lucky,

You probably wonder why your father did not make any attempt to enter into your life. I cannot explain it, except to say that he thought it was the right thing to do. He thought you would be happier not knowing him.

However, the contents of these two boxes represent his legacy. He earned his living as a technical translator, but this is what he loved. He wanted you to have these books.

If you are ever in Oregon, I hope you will come to see me. It would be a great pleasure to meet you.

Yours, Stick

29. something discovered about triple T

Lucky didn't get it. She pulled out three or four books and looked at the covers. They were adult novels and poetry collections by different authors she had never heard of. The jackets were boring and shabby and they smelled dusty. It was seriously disappointing, especially after she had built up in her mind how this gift, his only gift, was going to somehow reveal something important about her father. But it was just the books he'd had.

There were two short knocks on the front door and Pete's voice saying, "Lucky?" He stuck his head in. "Just wanted to say I was sorry to hear about your father."

Pete had come to help with the new kitchen cabin, and he'd been working over there with Brigitte, Klincke Ken, and Dot, installing shelves and cupboards. They were getting it ready for the Café's new opening the following weekend.

"Thanks." Lots of people had told her that it was lucky she

hadn't really known her father, as if that meant his death were less important, which made Lucky angry. She was grateful that Pete did not say this.

He came in carrying two oranges in one hand and a large white plastic bag in the other. He tossed one of the oranges to her. "Here, try this. From my tree in L.A." Pete drove up to Hard Pan more and more often, almost every weekend, and everyone knew it was because he liked not only Brigitte's cooking but Brigitte. Lucky benefited from this because Pete enjoyed Paloma's company for the three-hour trip, and Paloma's mother had quit worrying so much, so the girls were able to get together pretty often. But this was one weekend Paloma hadn't been able to come.

Lucky felt a little sad and a little crabby. She returned the books to the boxes and pushed them to the end of the table, against the wall. "Why do you think my father asked his sister to send me these books of his?" she asked Pete. "It's a horrible present."

He slid into the banquette opposite her and began to peel his orange, the plastic bag on the seat beside him. "Well, I guess that's the paradox. If you had known him, you'd know why. Maybe they're books he wanted you to read someday when you're older, books he liked a lot. They must have been important to him."

"Stick said that. She said they were his legacy to me." Lucky piled her own orange peels in a neat stack on the table.

"Speaking as a geologist, I know I wouldn't really understand until I looked inside," Pete said.

Lucky rolled her eyes. "Oh, please. Right now I'm almost done with a really good book called *Charles and Emma*. I don't want to read Triple T's old books."

"We need paper towels," Pete said, and got up to yank two off the roll. The trailer was filled with the scent of oranges. "I didn't say read them. Just have a look. Like, why these particular books? What is it about them that he liked so much?"

Lucky didn't want to know, but she *did* want to know. She frowned.

"Mind if I look?"

"I guess not," Lucky said. Yet she suddenly felt possessive of these books that she didn't want. It was weird.

Sometimes Pete had a silly aspect to him, as if there were a little boy hiding inside his grown-up body, and Lucky could imagine how cute he'd probably been, with very mischievous dark sparkly eyes, the kind of small boy whose mother is always laughing and flapping her dishcloth at him. He stuck an orange segment between his lips so that it looked like he had orange teeth. Lucky rolled her eyes at him again, but then she did the same with her own orange segment. As usual, his cheeks were dark because of his fast-growing beard. Lucky always wanted to touch those cheeks. Pete reached into the box.

"*Dying on the Vine: Nineteenth-Century French Poetry on Love and Death*, by Jean-Pierre de la St. Helene," he read, showing

Lucky the front cover of a large gray rectangle against a yellow background. He pulled out another book. *"Letters from Home: Correspondence Between the Duc d'Auvergne and His Daughter."* This jacket featured a photo of a bleak-looking mountain.

"See what I mean? Those both look, like, boring to the max."

Pete shrugged; he didn't disagree, but he said, "Maybe you'll appreciate them when you're older." He turned to the title page of the poetry book. "Whoa—check this out, Lucky." He passed it across the table to her and opened the other book.

"'Translated from the original French by Taggart Theodore Trimble,'" she read.

"He translated this one too. I bet these are all books he translated." He said, "Pretty obscure authors—there's probably not a very big readership for them."

Lucky considered. Her father had never talked to her except one time after her mother died. He had said the next decision would be hers, and it would be the right one. That was a strange thing to have said, but at the time she hadn't even known he was her father! If she had known, she'd have asked questions and tried to find out what he meant.

She thought about how he had spent his life translating words from one language to another. Perhaps it was his way, his only way, of saying something—through other people's thoughts. She turned to the next page in the poetry book. There was a little quote all alone on the page by someone called Edna St. Vincent Millay. It said, "Life must go on; I forget just why."

Those words seemed to tug at her; they made her want to curl up in someone's lap like a small child. *Maybe,* Lucky was thinking, *there are all kinds of heaven and all kinds of hell. And maybe we get a little taste of them even before we die, just like Lincoln said.*

She slid out from the table, walked over to Pete, and gave him a peck on his coarse-grade sandpaper cheek. She liked the way it felt. "I'm going to read them," she said. "Someday."

30. a masterful communication

On his way out, Pete said, "Oh, that stuff in the plastic bag—I saw it in the trash bin at work. Probably from some student project." Pete worked for Cal State Northridge as a geology professor. "Thought you might be able to use them, but they'll need some Windex first. Otherwise, you can just toss them."

Inside the large white plastic bag was a jumble of clear acrylic boxes of varying sizes, from small enough for a button to large enough for a football. Some of the plastic was a little scratched, and most of the boxes were smudged, but they were fine. The close-fitting lids revealed the purpose of these boxes to Lucky: They magnified the thing you put into each box.

Specimen boxes!

She sat there, resisting the strong urge to bring out her Altoids tins with their scorpions, tarantulas, ants, wasps, dragonflies, moths, and owl pellets, plus her mouse mummy and almost perfect snakeskin in an old shoe box. The snake had outgrown its skin and left it behind in a water meter box; it was one of her great treasures. The skin was as fragile as a butterfly wing and transparent and quite dry; it had to be handled carefully. She thought it would look magnificent coiled inside the largest box.

"Beag," she said to HMS Beagle. "Can you imagine how much Charles Darwin would have loved these specimen boxes? Can you *even imagine*?"

The Beag listened attentively, as she always did, because everything Lucky said was interesting and true and important. She got up from her rug, stretched out her neck, and thoroughly sniffed the boxes. She wagged her tail very slowly from side to side, a sign that she was intrigued. Lucky realized that the Beag probably knew, because of her exceptional sense of smell, exactly what the student had used them for, precisely what creatures had been inside those boxes.

The dog tucked her rear end neatly beneath her, sitting gracefully; then she shifted her weight from one front paw to the other and back again, her ears slightly raised, watching Lucky intently. Then she gazed at the door, then back at Lucky, then at the door. Without even thinking about it, Lucky translated: We should go OUT! OUT is good! Bugs and snakes are OUT! And birds! They are OUT also! I can catch them for you! Or chase them and let them get away! Or we can go OUT and just smell things! We really should go OUT!

Her dog, Lucky thought, was a masterful communicator.

Even if you were from the South Pole or the moon, you would know exactly what she was saying.

Lucky checked under the sink for the Windex and found a piece of old T-shirt in the clean rag corner. "Come on," she said. "Let's go out for a while before we start that project." The dog was already at the door. As Lucky opened it, she added, "I just hope Brigitte likes Pete as much as we do." HMS Beagle, flying down the steps after Lucky, thoroughly agreed.

31. two problems

Lucky had learned, through Miles, that Klincke Ken and Short Sammy had discussed the problem at length before they finally decided to consult Brigitte. They each carried a paper grocery sack, making their way on foot, grim but determined, to the kitchen trailer.

Hearing their approach, Lucky opened the door and Brigitte was right behind her. "Come in," Brigitte said. "We are almost ready for the grand opening, which is very soon. So what do you think of the new name: The Regulation Number 1849 Café?"

Klincke Ken and Short Sammy stared at Brigitte, speechless.

Brigitte laughed. "Oh, it is a joke. Do not look so worried! Stu Burping inspects the cooking cabin yesterday and Brigitte's Hard Pan Café has the new permit." She hugged Lucky from behind. "Every table has been reserved. You and Dot and the Captain are our guests of honor, of course."

Short Sammy tipped back his stained white hat as a gesture of respect, allowing Lucky to see his forehead's wavy horizontal creases, which were similar to the pattern of the corrugated tin of his water tank house roof. "Brigitte, we need help," he said.

"Anything! Tell me what you need."

"We need to go to ironing school," Klincke Ken explained.

"Ironing school? What is this?"

Klincke Ken pulled out a wadded-up shirt from his sack. "Can't come to the opening with our clothes in their normal way," he said. "So we tried ironing 'em, but we just plain can't do it right."

"They want you to teach them how to iron their shirts," Lucky explained.

"Ah! Of course!" Brigitte stepped aside so the two men could come inside.

183

"Here's our board we used," Short Sammy said, pulling a short wooden plank from his sack.

Brigitte made a *tsk* sound. "Lucky, can you bring out the ironing table and the iron? We cannot use this little piece of wood."

A few minutes later, Miles stuck his head in the door as Brigitte began demonstrating how to lay out the sleeve and spray it with a little water. The two men leaned over the shirt, paying close attention. Lucky put a finger to her lips and gestured for Miles to follow her into her canned-ham trailer.

"Is Paloma here yet?" he whispered.

"Not yet. What's up?"

"Nothing." He let himself fall forward onto his knees next to HMS Beagle, then he lay down beside her on the rug, one arm draped over her body. She raised her head briefly, then let it drop back down.

"Wow, you guys are pretty lively."

"Don't be ironic right now, okay, Lucky?"

They heard Short Sammy asking whether it was really important to iron all around each button, since the other side, the side of the shirt with the button*holes*, covered up all that cloth around the buttons. Couldn't you just let it stay wrinkled where nobody would see? They heard the iron being parked firmly on Brigitte's board. They heard Brigitte ask, "It is important? Of course it is important if you want to do this ironing the right way. I thought that is what you are coming to find out!"

They heard both men agreeing, yes, that was exactly what they came to find out, and would she please continue with the lesson.

Lucky wandered over to her porthole window, the one that gave out onto the Café tables and beyond them to the Mojave Desert. She opened it, and the scent of sage and creosote came in, mingling with the smell of boy and dog. The worry she had had before—it used to come at odd moments, about going to Einstein Junior High in a few weeks—was mostly gone now. Ollie had announced that he would be, kind of, her sponsor. This happened very rarely in junior high, especially between a famous popular ninth-grade skateboarder and a nonathletic unpopular seventh-grade scientist, and Lucky was grateful. He said he would make sure nobody bullied her, although she was already pretty good at dealing with that situation herself, and he'd help her find her classrooms if she wanted. He said she shouldn't sit with him at lunch, but she could if it was an emergency. Lucky found this very generous.

And in a few days Brigitte's Hard Pan Café would have its grand reopening; they'd prepared for it all week. Sandi the bus driver signed on to be an additional server. Stick had sent a gift: a spectacular restaurant-style dishwasher; it washed, sterilized, and dried dishes in just a few minutes. Dot was going to bring flowers from her garden, and Justine would make bouquets in tiny spice jar vases for each table. There would probably be at least three seatings, a very busy day, and the same again on Sunday. The fridge in the new kitchen cabin would soon be

filled with desserts, salad ingredients, and the makings for all the blackboard menu dishes. They were nearly ready.

And yet Lucky didn't feel ready, and she didn't know what she wasn't ready *for*.

Out of nowhere, Miles said, "It's not that we don't believe in evolution."

Surprised, Lucky said, "Really? What made you think of that all of a sudden?"

He didn't answer. Lucky sat on the bed and placed her socked feet very gently against his back. "Like a virus can evolve into a stronger virus," he explained finally. "A species of bird can adapt, over time, by its beak getting longer or whatever. But one species cannot evolve into another species."

"So . . . ?"

"So we're not related to the other primates. We didn't evolve from a common ancestor."

"Ah."

Lucky knew that prior to Justine's return, Miles had read

a zillion books about dinosaurs and early hominids. She poked him gently with her big toes.

Miles continued, "If it weren't for God, I wouldn't have a mom. He saved her, and he brought her back here. I say prayers about that a lot, every day. But some of my questions I can't ask God about, like what will happen in school."

"You mean if your teacher says something and it goes against the Bible?"

"Yeah."

"Your mom should go in and talk with Ms. Baum-Izzart, so she can let your teacher know that you have different beliefs."

"She's checking to see what all she has to do for me to be homeschooled."

"Uck. You'd have to spend your whole entire life in Hard Pan and never see any other kids."

"Well, she says we could have field trips once she gets her driver's license, when Grandma doesn't need the car, and maybe she'll meet other moms in some of the outlying towns or in Sierra City, and we could all be homeschooled together."

"Hmm."

"Lucky, it's kind of hard. I love God, and I know Jesus loves me, but I hate maybe not being able to go to school and read regular books, and I hate having to *not* believe things I'm pretty sure are really true, like things in science." Miles raised up on one arm, looking at Lucky. His face was angry and sad and hopeful all at the same time.

"Well, listen, Miles. Even though you're a kid, you're still a person. You can decide things. Maybe your decision right now is to keep learning everything about the Bible."

"I can already recite a ton of verses by heart."

"I know. It's amazing. But anyway, think about this: You could make your own choice to keep on doing that, not because anyone forces you but because it's what you decide. Then *later* you can make up your mind about dinosaurs. *Later* you can read all you want about science. But right now, maybe you could decide to stick with the Bible. See what I mean?" She jiggled him with her toes. He didn't answer.

She said, "Just keep thinking with your brain like you always do. You don't have to say everything you think out loud. And the other thing is, remember that Justine is still a beginner mom, like Brigitte was my beginner mom. Trust me, they really don't know what they're doing at first. But the big thing is that Justine loves you. No matter what, she loves you and she's trying her best. And your grandmother, too. Maybe they're driving each other crazy because they each want different things for you." Then Lucky added softly, "So maybe *you* have to be the one to cut some slack."

"That almost sounds like something out of the Bible."

"Well, I don't know about that. Maybe. But here's what I think: Right now it's the grown-ups' world. But later *we'll* be the grown-ups and it'll be *our* world and we'll be able to do anything we want. We can fix things then."

Miles gazed at her. "Lucky," he said, "if it's okay with Lincoln, I mean if you'd rather it was Lincoln, that would be okay too, but—" He reddened, then went on in a rush. "Could we get married? I mean when we're grown up. We could both be scientists together."

"Miles, that's my very first proposal, and I'm not even twelve yet. I'm, I don't know, honored. Let's think about it for a while . . . like twenty years or so, okay?"

"Sure," he said, and hugged HMS Beagle.

When Lucky got up to look out her window again, she saw Klincke Ken and Short Sammy walking away, each holding an ironed shirt on a wire hanger. One was very short, in cowboy boots and hat; the other, wearing bib overalls and construction-worker boots, a foot taller. They walked in a peppier way than when they'd arrived, like people who had faced a troubling problem head-on and resolved it with just a little help from a friend.

32. climbing upstairs to heaven

Lucky had caught on that things hardly ever turn out the way you expect. For instance, once Justine finished making her *Climbing Upstairs to Heaven* sculpture out of bird and rodent bones regurgitated by owls, she became famous.

Well, famous in a Hard Pan kind of way. When word about the sculpture got around, everyone wanted to see it. Mrs. Prender had set it up on its own little table right in the living room of her double-wide, where it got the morning sun. The sanded and lacquered Popsicle-stick platform base measured about a foot square; it was raised up to form a pedestal by more layers of interwoven Popsicle sticks underneath. In its center was a spiral staircase, so well proportioned and structurally sound that you knew immediately what it was. A person about the height of a Popsicle stick could have climbed those stairs, curving around and around, gliding along with a hand lightly on the railing.

The staircase itself drew people closer, as they realized that all the lacy filigree steps and the railing, everything but the central pole, which was a stainless-steel barbecue skewer, all were made from tiny bones intricately fit together and invisibly glued. It looked impossible, like a DNA pattern. And it had an airiness, a lightness that made people take in their breath and want to touch it, to feel the tiny smooth bones that looked, on close examination, so much like certain human bones.

So when the Wellbornes came to Hard Pan for a visit, Lucky and Paloma brought them straight to Mrs. Prender's. Mrs. Wellborne was on the board of a famous art museum in Brentwood, and she had admired the small oil paintings, painted by Lucky's mother Lucille, that were displayed in the new kitchen cabin. They figured Mrs. Wellborne would be blown away by Justine's *Climbing Upstairs to Heaven*.

But they were wrong. It wasn't Mrs. Wellborne, though she did like it very much. No, it was Mr. Wellborne who was over-the-top captivated. He walked around it five or six times. He bent down, his nose almost touching, for a close look. He asked for a step stool in order to look straight down on it. Lucky was very proud of her own role in gathering the pellets and dissecting them so that Justine would have the materials she needed, and she never tired of telling visitors how she had done this. (Mrs. Wellborne wanted to know, like all other adults, whether she'd washed her hands after handling the pellets, and she assured Pal's mom—with only the barest hint of irony—that she had.)

"Well, Ms. Prender," Mr. Wellborne said at last. Justine, sitting off to the side, looked up. Lucky stared at her, puzzling because there was something different, until she realized what it was. Justine's hands rested on the arms of the chair and her feet rested on the floor. She was totally relaxed and calm, not a twitch, tap, or jiggle. Lucky frowned. She figured Justine must be so, so scared about the Wellbornes examining her staircase that it almost paralyzed her. But then Justine smiled a radiant, confident, trustful smile. She did not look one bit worried or nervous. Mr. Wellborne smiled back at her. "I don't know if you're interested in selling this piece," he said, "or if you have any others, but I guarantee I know at least three producers who would buy it. You could name your price."

192

"It's not for sale," Justine said. "I'm going to give it to the Found Object Wind Chime Museum and Visitor Center, if the museum wants it."

"Well, how about making some other bone sculptures? This is an exciting piece of art, Ms. Prender. You should get yourself an agent."

"He's right, dear," Mrs. Wellborne said. "You should."

Justine shook her head. The light streaming in the window lit her from behind, so she looked as if she wore a glowing spiky-haired halo, like a really strange angel. This made Lucky wonder about angels as an aspect of evolution—like maybe during the time people were evolving a bigger brain, angels were evolving a bigger capacity for grace, that quality Justine sometimes mentioned. Lucky wished Lincoln were there so she could discuss this with him. Lincoln, in fact, now that she thought about it, probably had an angel among *his* ancestors, somewhere on his family tree, maybe one of his great-greats. If that were true, she decided, then angels might not even know they were angels.

Justine was saying, "No, I already have one. Jesus is my agent."

After a moment Mr. Wellborne said, "Well! None better! Then we'll come back and visit your work here in Hard Pan at the museum, right, Carmen? We hope there will be more to see."

193

"A mosaic is what I'm imagining," Justine said. "Quite large."

"What's a mosaic?" Paloma asked.

Mrs. Wellborne said, "You've seen them in Rome, dear, in some of the cathedrals. Where they take little pieces of stone or pottery or shells and fit them together to make a picture. It's a very ancient art. So," she said to Justine, "would this be a floor mosaic?"

"No, it'll be on a wall, I think. A mural about ten feet high by twenty or thirty feet across."

"Good heavens!" Mr. Wellborne exclaimed. "That's incredible! Is there a wall that big that you can use inside the museum?"

"What I envision," Justine said, dipping her head to the side and squinting a little at the ceiling, "is an outside wall, facing west, facing the setting sun."

Mr. Wellborne stared out the window, hands clasped behind his back. He turned around. "May I ask what materials you're thinking of for this mosaic? Stone, I would guess, since there's rather a lot of it around."

Justine slowly shook her head. "No. I was thinking glass. There are shards and pieces of broken glass all over the desert. Different colors, some of it quite old glass, but lasting, and there would be that shining effect when the sun hits the surface. Wait, I'll give you an idea of how it'll look." She reached behind her to a shelf and pulled off a spiral notebook. Peering over her shoulder as Justine flipped through, Lucky could see that it was filled with pencil drawings. "Here's a rough idea of the design," Justine said, folding back the notebook at a particular page and handing it to Mr. Wellborne.

The Wellbornes studied the drawing for some time, and then they exchanged a look, raising their eyebrows. "My word," Mr. Wellborne said softly. Mrs. Wellborne gazed from the drawing to him and back. "Absolutely," she agreed, and they nodded at each other. He handed the notebook back to Justine. "This is exceptionally powerful. But won't it be dangerous, working with pieces of broken glass?"

"I'll be careful. But I'm not worried—I know I'll be safe."

"Indeed. Yes. Well, Carmen and I may be of assistance, Ms.

Prender. Our foundation provides work-in-progress grants for extremely promising film students and occasionally for artists in other media. Based on your sculpture and the sketch of the wall mosaic, we're interested in helping. I'm referring to a grant that would support you and your son while you do the new project. No strings attached. No strings whatsoever."

Lucky bugged out her eyes at Paloma, who bugged hers out back at Lucky.

"Well," Justine said, her eyes shining. "Thank you. I guess my agent will consider that an amazing and very generous offer."

Lucky wanted to get to a private place so she and Paloma could thoroughly discuss this. Ever since Justine had come, Lucky worried that she would not stay long in Hard Pan; that she would want to take Miles to a real city where they had churches. But now she knew she needn't have been concerned, for Justine had plenty in common with others in their little town: She had her own definite ideas about things, and she knew what she wanted, and she didn't care one bit what anybody thought. Lucky realized she was going to fit into Hard Pan just fine. Justine was going to stay.

33. serenity

No one would have been able to visit the museum to which Justine wanted to give her sculpture were it not for Short Sammy DeSoto, volunteer docent, who kept the key on a nail on an outside wall of his water tank house. It was Short Sammy who wiped fingerprints off the display cases, swept the floor, and related stories about the old mining days to tourists. But now he told the Captain, who told Klincke Ken, who told Mrs. Prender, that he wasn't sure if he wanted to keep on being the town's only docent if he now had to be responsible for such a valuable sculpture.

Henrietta had sort of an answer to Short Sammy's concern over responsibility for Justine's sculpture, because of his being the one in charge of the key to the museum. She had worked for many years for the county government and therefore knew a great deal about committees and meetings, and on the subject of the key to the museum she declared that there should be a committee and that it should hold a meeting. Reluctantly, Henrietta herself (since it had been her idea) agreed to join the committee, along with Short Sammy, Dot, and, at the Captain's suggestion, Lucky Trimble.

Lucky loved serving on the Hard Pan Museum Key Committee because it was a little like being in the principal's office without being in trouble. Her opinions and ideas were listened to just as much as those of the adult committee members. It was Lucky's idea to summon Justine to the meeting as a consultant, in order to ask her why she had refused to sell the sculpture. The reason the committee needed this information was simply that everyone wanted badly to know. If she'd sold it, she'd be rich, *and* the town wouldn't be facing this museum key problem.

Justine told them: She said she gave it to the museum in order to help her to comprehend the idea of serenity. Privately, Lucky noticed, as she had before with the Wellbornes, that Justine already *was* more serene—or at least a lot less fidgety. So Lucky didn't get it, unless maybe to Justine serenity meant something different. Short Sammy looked up from under the brim of his hat and said, "'The courage to change the things I can.'"

"Yes," Justine responded.

"Just for today," Short Sammy said. Justine nodded. Lucky figured that this was code talk about recovering from addictions. Because of having eavesdropped on twelve-step meetings when she was younger, she was able, sort of, to follow the conversation. Henrietta said, "Well, we'll just keep working on this key problem, then," and Justine thanked them and left.

It turned out that they needed a second meeting, as Henrietta had darkly predicted from the start. At that meeting, the committee members presented their reports, having canvassed all residents of the Hard Pan community to see if anyone else was willing to take over the job of museum docent, or at least share it. It turned out that no one was. So the committee recommended that at some point another committee should be convened to write a grant proposal requesting funding for a paid permanent part-time Found Object Wind Chime Museum and Visitor Center attendant.

But nobody had time to take on any more committee work at the moment, so the key remained hanging on the nail outside of Short Sammy's water tank house, and the sculpture remained in Mrs. Prender's front room, where anybody could go and see it anyway.

And Lucky noticed when she was there that Miles hung around the sculpture more than anyone, studying the staircase carefully, as if it would tell him what he needed to know.

34. lucky for good

Lucky had tried many times in the past, because of school
assignments in fourth and fifth grade, to like poetry. She read it
aloud as her teachers recommended, and she tried writing her
own. Nothing worked, and she always went back gratefully to
books about bugs and animals and her hero, Charles Darwin.
But now Lucky was reading a book of poetry her father, Triple
T, had translated. Even though she didn't understand it in a
complete, thorough, scientific way, many of the lines seemed
to give off reflections, as if covered by tiny mirrors; they shim-
mered in her brain.

Although he hadn't written the poems, they connected her
with her father. As she read them, she knew that he had handled
each word, turning it to the light or putting it to his ear to find
out if it breathed. Lucky liked the idea of her father doing this,
examining words the way she examined specimens.

These thoughts about being linked in an unexpected way
with Triple T made her brood over her family tree.

The project had revealed to whom she was officially biologically connected, but Lucky considered it to be false and incomplete. Neatly recorded were the names of her ancestors, including all eight great-grands, which she'd found with the help of Mrs. Kennedy and Stick. Ms. Baum-Izzart was pleased and said she'd done a fine job. But to Lucky it was mostly just a tree full of strangers, stiff and lifeless. Her principal gave it back to her and told her to keep it in a safe place.

"It's mine now? Mine for good?"

"Of course, Lucky. It's your family."

So Lucky added new branches. On one she wrote, HMS BEAGLE, DOG. On another, SIOBHAN TRIMBLE KELLY (STICK).

She drew a thick branch between her maternals and her paternals. On it she wrote Brigitte's name, and Brigitte's parents', sisters', and grandparents' names. Now her tree seemed to thrum with life, like the actual Joshua tree in the dry creek bed behind her trailer that lodged families of lizards, pocket mice, cactus wrens, and beautiful small white moths.

Still, it wasn't finished, because in Lucky's opinion a family tree should have the family of your blood *and* the family of your heart *and* the family of your secret deep-inside self. So she went back online to the runes website. Using the chart there, she wrote in Elder Futhark near the trunk of her tree,

LINCOLN CLINTON CARTER KENNEDY

MILES PRENDER

PALOMA WELLBORNE

SHORT SAMMY DESOTO

CHARLES DARWIN

She had to make up a rune for *C* in order to do this, but she didn't think the ancient Vikings would mind. Down by where the tree's roots would be, she added ANNIE DARWIN, her future daughter. She thought for a long time about how to include her Higher Power, and then she finally inscribed, in tiny runes along the top and sides of the page,

OH GOD OF OUR MANY UNDERSTANDINGS:

In all the rush and hard work of preparing for the Café's opening, Lucky thought she'd misplaced her new family tree, or that it had gotten mixed up with some other paperwork or something, because it went missing for a while. But the next time Pete came to visit he handed it to her, under glass and framed in delicate carved wood. This made it look unexpectedly beautiful, like an intricate work of art. Brigitte took it from Lucky and stood gazing at it in her two outstretched hands, and then she hugged it, twirling around in her bare feet, and then she hung it in her new kitchen cabin among the paintings by Lucille.

It was nearly the end of summer, the months of brief and sudden rainstorms, the time of brash winds and flash floods. Evenings vibrated with the racket of insects shouting *What if! What if! What if!* at the tops of their tiny wings and legs and lungs. And each afternoon the ferocious sun, pouring red and gold, seemed to waver before it plunged behind the Coso mountains, as if reluctant to leave.

A long time ago, after her mother Lucille had died, Lucky worried a lot about changes, and she had tried to be ready for anything at all times with her survival kit backpack. She worried about losing her way.

Now Lucky suspected that she would be able to manage. It seemed that someone, often herself, always needed to be rescued in Hard Pan, but now she knew that sometimes she would be the one who would come *to* the rescue.

And another new thing: She liked the way life was always changing; she felt a kind of zinging excitement about it. Tomorrow was the opening, the reopening, of Brigitte's Hard Pan Café. And in a few weeks, the start of junior high. Those new beginnings felt like the blast of bright light when you're inside on a summer day and you open the door—it blinds you for a second, being so powerful, but you're suddenly brimming with courage, braver than you knew you could be, even as you take your first step out, your whole life waiting for you in the vast shimmering world.

♣

acknowledgments

Caitlyn Dlouhy combines feistiness, clarity, vision, kindness, and humor in one terrific package marked Editor. Thank you, Caitlyn. And thanks, too, to Kiley Frank for her keen eye and excellent ear.

205

Grateful thanks to Dr. Steven Chun for pediatric medical advice and other useful suggestions; to Nordine Patron for his candor and insights on school-yard and principal-office dynamics; to Ben Chun; to Erin Miskey for references and information regarding the Bible and Christian apologetics, and for painstakingly responding to several drafts; to Eva Cox and Rob Robbins for enthusiastic responses when most needed; to Lindsey Philpott of the International Guild of Knot Tyers for once again lending his knotting expertise; to my *belle-soeur* Liliane Moussy for giving me time to write by doing the cooking; to Gandalf for showing me everything I needed to know about the Beag (RIP, good dog); and to Lloyd Woolever for photos, a video, and his eyewitness account of a house being moved in a way very similar to the event described here. Thanks to Lloyd, also, for sharing his story of ironing school.

Patricia Leavengood and Georgia Chun read draft versions of this book and sent thoughtful comments. As always, I'm awed by their bigheartedness and moral support.

Pal to my Lucky, Theresa Nelson gave her (and me) more writerly help than I can ever repay. We're hatched from the same egg, to my everlasting gratitude. Additional thanks to Virginia Walter and Lucy Frank, my fine writing friends.

The Hard Pan trilogy has enjoyed a trilogy of the finest editors in the field: Richard Jackson, Ginee Seo, and Caitlyn Dlouhy. How lucky I have been, and how extremely grateful.

As always, Ernie Nortap gave me my best lines (charging only ten dollars each), loaded the dishwasher, squeezed the orange juice, and understood the intricacies, challenges, and craziness inherent in this work.

notes to the reader

Charts to convert English words into runes may be found at NOVA online: pbs.org/wgbh/nova/vikings/runes.html.

Lucky reads about Charles Darwin and his wife in *Charles and Emma: The Darwins' Leap of Faith* by Deborah Heiligman (Holt, 2009).

The story of heaven and hell appears in the folklore of many cultures. George Shannon's retelling can be found in *Stories to Solve: Folktales from Around the World* (Greenwillow, 1985).

The writer Donald Westlake died on December 31, 2009, while I was writing this book. The chapter in the principal's office is an homage to Westlake, and especially to his Dortmunder comic capers.

The little quote Lucky finds in one of the fictional books her father translated, "Life must go on; I forget just why," is from the poem "Lament" by Edna St. Vincent Millay.

Justine's religious beliefs and her understanding of Biblical citations are all her own and do not represent those of any person or group.

ᛟᚾ ᚷᛟᛞ ᛟᚠ ᛟᚢᚱ ᛈᚪᛋᛏ ᚾᛁᛞᛟᛗᚱᛋᛏᚪᛞᛁᛟᛋ

The Higher Power of Lucky,
Lucky Breaks,
and *Lucky for Good*
Reading Group Guide

1. Lucky, Lincoln, and Miles are the only kids in Hard Pan. Describe their relationship. Miles is especially annoying to Lucky. Do you think it's his age, his personality, or the echo of him in her own longing for a mom that sometimes irritates her? Discuss the circumstances that change the relationship of the three kids as they grow a little older in *Lucky Breaks* and *Lucky for Good*.

2. In *The Higher Power of Lucky*, Lucky eavesdrops at the anonymous twelve-step meetings at the museum and learns that each person is in search of a Higher Power. Discuss why Lucky is so anxious to find her Higher Power. The twelve-step people tell about rock-bottom moments before finding their Higher Power. What is Lucky's rock-bottom moment? Explain why the "getting in control of your life" step is especially difficult for Lucky. At what point in the novel does Lucky discover her Higher Power? How does discovering it set her life on a different course?

3. Lucky's father asked Brigitte to take care of Lucky until she could be placed in a foster home. Brigitte says that she would want a foster home that would give Lucky a little freedom but some discipline as well. Discuss whether Brigitte offers this type of home environment for Lucky. Brigitte is a "beginning mom" in *The Higher Power of Lucky*. Describe Brigitte's mom skills by the end of *Lucky for Good*.

4. At the end of *The Higher Power of Lucky*, Lucky asks Brigitte, "What is a scrotum?" Discuss the symbolism in her question. What is symbolic about Lucky plugging up the knothole in the fence of the museum?

5. The three kids in Hard Pan are free to roam their desert town. How does freedom require responsibility? Discuss moments in all three novels when Lucky takes her freedom a little too far. How is learning to be responsible part of growing up? In *Lucky Breaks*, Lucky wants to be intrepid. How does she confuse acting intrepid with acting responsible? Discuss moments in the novels when Lucky is responsible. What is her most intrepid moment?

6. Abandonment is a central theme in all three novels. In *The Higher Power of Lucky*, Lucky is dealing with the death of her mother and with a father who doesn't want her. Debate whether Brigitte's decision to adopt her changes Lucky's feelings of abandonment. Miles's mother is in jail. Why does he think his situation is better than Lucky's?

7. Explain the following metaphor in *Lucky Breaks*: "She felt unseen, a lamp with its cord unplugged from the socket." Why does Lucky feel misunderstood? What doesn't she understand about herself? What more does she need and want? Debate whether she is searching for a more typical or ordinary life. At what point in *Lucky for Good* does Lucky finally feel that her "cord is plugged into the socket"?

8. In *Lucky for Good*, Lucky elects to research her family tree as punishment for fighting Ollie Martin. Why is the school principal worried about Lucky taking on this particular assignment? How does the assignment help Lucky discover her family? Why did her father want her to have his books upon his death? Debate whether Lucky can now deal with the feelings of abandonment that have plagued her for so long.

9. Lucky and Lincoln have been best friends forever. Now that Lucky is growing up, she really wants a girl friend. Describe the friendship that develops between Lucky and Paloma in *Lucky Breaks*. Discuss the term "polar opposites." How are Lucky and Paloma polar opposites? What is it that intrigues Paloma the most about Lucky's life in Hard Pan?

10. In *Lucky Breaks*, Paloma's mother isn't sure about letting her daughter spend the weekend in Hard Pan. Discuss Brigitte's conversation with Mrs. Wellborne about trust. Discuss the good and bad choices that Lucky and Paloma make. What

do they learn from their mistakes? What does Mrs. Wellborne discover about Hard Pan?

11. At first, Lucky thinks that she has to give up her friendship with Lincoln in order to have Paloma as a friend. What does Paloma help her realize about Lincoln? How does Lucky and Lincoln's relationship deepen by the end of Lucky for Good?

12. In *Lucky for Good*, the three kids from Hard Pan encounter Ollie Martin, a bully from Einstein Jr. High School. How are they unprepared for dealing with a bully? What is wrong in Ollie's life that causes him to be a bully? Discuss how he is eventually pulled into the circle of friends in Hard Pan.

13. Lincoln Clinton Carter Kennedy is named for four US Presidents. Based on his name, to which political party do you think his parents belong? Lucky thinks that Lincoln sounds and acts like a future president—grave, serious, and diplomatic. Discuss moments in each book when Lincoln displays each of these characteristics.

14. The Inyo County Health Department of the State of California wants to shut down Brigitte's Hard Pan Café because the kitchen is in a residence. How does the entire town engage in a solution to the problem?

15. Justine, Miles's mom, returns from prison a changed woman. How does her newly discovered religion confuse Miles?

Debate whether she was part of a twelve-step program in prison. Mrs. Prender and Justine argue about religion. Debate how Miles might view religion as he becomes an adult.

16. Justine thinks that Lucky is a "sinner" for studying Charles Darwin and the theory of evolution. And she won't allow Miles to read the dinosaur books that he has always enjoyed. Why is Justine so afraid of what Miles is reading? Mrs. Prender reminds Justine that Miles is considered a gifted child. Discuss whether Justine is frightened by Miles's intelligence. How is censorship a form of mind control? Explain what Lucky means when she advises Miles to keep thinking with his "own brain." How is "thinking with your own brain" a healthy way of dealing with the world around you?

17. Discuss how Susan Patron uses humor in characters and plot to reveal serious and profound themes.

18. At the end of *Lucky for Good*, Lucky realizes that there is always someone in Hard Pan who needs rescuing. She knows that she will sometimes be that person, and sometimes she will be the person that comes to the rescue. Trace Lucky's journey from needing to be rescued in *The Higher Power of Lucky* to her role as rescuer in *Lucky for Good*.